Town On Fire

Untold Stories from a Caribbean Coup

I0692391

Otancia Noel

Black Stone Press & DMC Books

© copyright 2025

Otancia Noel and Black Stone Press

ISBN: 9781838119065

http://opentrade.org.uk/black-stone-press/

Contents

Foreword

Otancia Noel's wonderful fictional collection Town on Fire, is based around the 1990 coup event in Trinidad and Tobago and explores the complexity of life for various individuals. The author draws on her own experiences of growing up on The Jamaat Al Muslimeen Compound in Trinidad and also being the daughter of someone who was involved in the 1990 coup attempt.

However, her literary skills and imaginative mind allow us to look at these events in particular, but life in general from a perspective that we may never have realised existed. It is no wonder that she has achieved so many awards and accolades (see credits).

The main thread in most of the stories is The Compound, The Khalif and Abi, and an exploration of life before the coup and after. The themes in the stories highlight culture, family ties, man's need for power, greed, abuse, rape, flawed leadership in the name of God, religious fanaticism, the psychological bond between leaders and their followers, the issue of internal migration in families moving to The Compound, external migration with the exodus of nationals to Syria all these elements are linked to The Compound.

Stories are shared from within and moves with how the compound and the characters were shaped. *Keturah* and others weaving stories about their family, like her father's second marriage in *Bam Bam See Am Look Thing* and on The Khalif's persona and stories about other members that we are immersed into this life, its legacy, its unravelling.

There are three stories that are not connected to the others, two folklore tales Pretty *Sue, Rahim and Papa Bois* and one about *The Village Santiwah*. The author dedicates these three stories to her grandmother who she credits with teaching her the art form of traditional oral storytelling. This book is testimony to her grandmother's prowess as a teacher and to Noel's own dedication as a student.

In the credits at the end of the book you will see that some of these stories were previously published as short stories winning the author many great accolades and awards.

The author has expressed her immense gratitude to the publishers, magazines, awarding bodies, judges and all the great individuals involved, as well as for all the feedback, advice and opportunities to travel that have resulted from all of that.

Amal Abdalhakim-Douglas
(February, 2025)

Author of: **Call of the Twice Removed** - The Role of the African/Caribbean in the Americas, Europe and Beyond

(But if you wanted to come find me,
{though I know I shouldn't}
I'm filling the ocean with stones you can step on,
all the way to my horizon)

..

Abdulmajeed Abdalkarim

Public Lies, Private Lives

At 21, Ace Hislop was easily the youngest ever recipient of the coveted Reporter of the Year Award. His winning entry, 'An Untold Story of an Uncool Coup', had garnered both the major prize along with a smaller prize for Best Feature Story.

But he did not feel as elated as one would have expected. Keturah's absence lay heavily on him. Had she been there in person to congratulate him, share the moment with him, it would have made this March night indisputably the best of his short professional life.

He remembered that day in front of the Red House on Abercromby Street when Keturah had first snarled at him when he stepped on her toes as he sought to find the best angle for his photo.

"Oh fock! Yuh cyar look way yuh putting yuh foot, asshole?"

"Oh, I beg your pardon," he apologized, jumping back, almost dropping his camera. "I'm sorry. I really am. I was just trying to get into the best possible position to take a photograph. Are you okay?"

She grimaced. "It eh go kill mih," she said. "But I wearing slippers and you not focking light."

"I'd kiss your feet if I thought that would make it better," he said.

He imagined a smile below the folds of cloth that masked her features, replacing the scowl that he was sure had, for the last couple of minutes, ruled them. At any rate, the absence of aggression, of truculence, in her body language suggested that her mood had softened

"Hey," he said, "let me make it up to you; let me buy you a drink. What would you like?"

"I would like you to stay off my foot," she joked, confirming his suspicions. "That would be a good place to start."

"No," he insisted. "I owe you one for literally stepping on your corns."

"I am a Muslim woman," she said, pulling herself up to her full 5' 4" height and looking almost disdainfully up at him. "You seriously expect me to take a drink with a perfect stranger?"

"I'm Ace Hislop," he said, extending his right hand, oblivious to the intended slight, "and I'm a *ClearCut* reporter. So now that you know my name and we're no longer strangers, shall we?"

She said nothing, and he suddenly realized she had made no move to accept his handshake. He felt slightly ashamed; which self-respecting reporter does not know that Muslim women never shake hands?

"You is a reporter?" she asked after a moment. He nodded. "A real reporter?"

He nodded again, reaching into his shirt pocket, and pulling out his *ClearCut* ID, which he held up for her to see.

"That is a real coincidence!" she said. "I think I want that drink, oui. Yuh offer still on?"

"Yes, of course," he said. "Let me just take my picture. Make sure your foot is out of the way and we're good to go."

Woodford Square, at the best of times, is not a place for a private conversation. The hard wooden benches line highly trafficked walkways criss-crossing the square and they are dirty from indiscriminate use by indiscriminate people. Today was a bad day to be in the Square because, apart from it being Friday, it was month's end and the last day of the school year. Uniformed schoolchildren were everywhere, and the crowd was unbearably thick.

Young in age and young in business, Ace was, however, an old hand at navigating crowds. He steered his newfound friend expertly towards Frederick Street and then down to Centre City

Mall. They settled into a pair of facing seats at the food court and their one-on-one began. She found out that he had done well at school, loved his job, and adored his father. He found out that her name was Keturah AI-Haqq, sensed that she had lost someone close to her in the now 25-year-old aborted coup d'état and suspected that she hated her father. He had decided she *must have* an interesting story to tell.

"I wasn't even born," he told her, settling back into his place on the upholstered bench and passing her the thick straw he had just come back from fetching, "when ANR Robinson and the NAR came to power. But Dad hated that pair with a passion, and I have heard many, many stories from him about Robbie and Club 88 and the ten percent salary cut and VAT." He raised his glass of passion fruit and took a long swig. "And" he continued, "about The Khalif and 1990."

"You ent hear my story," she mumbled. "Nobody ent hear my story."

Ace felt a thrill of satisfaction run down his spine. When he had impulsively offered to buy her a drink, he hadn't the slightest inkling that this lady swathed in cloth from head to toe might be a rich lode to tap into. Now, here she was about to tell him some story that with luck, he could use in the 25th Anniversary Special his paper was preparing.

"…I'll be 43 tomorrow," she was saying, almost to herself. "Forty-three. He didn't even reach 20."

"Who?" Ace asked, bursting with curiosity but wary about pushing too hard so as not to staunch her flow even before it began, not to drive her back into herself

"Khalid, meh big brother. They kill him in the Red House."

She went silent, sucking on the invisible straw behind her nikhab.

"So, he was just 18?" Ace prodded after a while, trying to get her started again.

"They kill him three weeks after he eighteenth birthday."

Smiling and showing the two dimples, his mother always said would melt any woman's heart, Ace asked: "Can I record this?"

She shrugged. He took that as an affirmative and started the recorder and put it on the table between them. "Go on," he said. "It's on."

As he was about to reach for his camera, she reached out her hand to prevent him. "No," she said, "no pictures."

He frowned. "Please, just one."

"No pictures," she repeated.

"Fine. No pictures," he said to her. And to himself.

"I remember it like it was yesterday," she began, "walking home from the Government School and picking sticky banga, grugru bef, pois doux and jackfruit. We use to linger in Las Palance, the ghetto area, to play hopscotch with my friend Ann-Marie, who father was my father good friend. Ann-Marie was a coco panyol, light-skin with a round face and a straight nose and big, moonshape, hazelnut-colour eyes. Khalid did like she bad, bad, and we use to spend plenty time playing with she."

She paused. "Them was good times," she continued, "We was young and free. It didn't last."

She explained that the friendship had endured, but the good times had not. Then, in the 1980s, when she had left school in the area, she and Ann-Marie had drifted apart. Later, after Ann-Marie's brother's death resulted in her mother being sent to St. Ann's, she found herself alone with a "wayward father." A few months after the coup, the police had raided Ann-Marie's family house one evening, looking for arms and ammunition her father was supposed to have. Right at the beginning of the raid, they had shot her brother as he was coming down the stairs. Her mother had lost her marbles and ended up in the psychiatric hospital in St. Ann's. Anne-Marie, neglected by her bandit father, had slid easily into prostitution.

"The papers say that how he shoot at the police," Keturah explained. And Ace imagined her eyes ablaze with anger behind her tinted lenses. "But that was a frigging lie! He hand was on the bannister as he was coming down the stairs and the police rush in and shoot him in he chest and he head in front ah he mother. Ann-Marie see everything, and she tell me the whole story."

"We did own a big, sprawling house in the middle ah Arma not far from the old racetrack..." "One second," he interrupted, stopping the recorder. "You sure you don't want to tell me the entire story?"

"I could link yuh up with Ann-Marie if yuh want Ann-Marie story," she laughed.

"Fair enough," Ace conceded. "Go ahead. Tell it your way." He pressed the record button.

"What I was saying? Oh yes, the house in Arma. We had a big house on Loubon Street in Arma, not far from the market. But we use to spend most ah the time with we grandmother, four ah we, me, Khalid, meh sister Jasmine, who we use to call 'Bones', and the baby

15

Hamidullah, who we use to call 'Ham'. My mother and my wotliss father was never home. She was taking classes in Sando and he used to drive truck and maxi and he was always in town with the Islamic Party."

Her grandparents owned an enormous estate with lots of fruit trees in Arma, not too far east of Palo near the heliport. There were mangoes, oranges, grapefruits, Chile and Governor plums, sapodillas, and a complete section devoted to vegetables as well. Her grandmother, she said, loved flowers and plants and cultivated them in abundance on the estate. Rare and lovely orchids abounded, as did palms, roses, crotons, hibiscus of every variety and hue, vervain, Christmas bush, Wonder of the World and an abundance of flora and fauna graced this wonderland.

Was she telling him this, Ace wondered, because she didn't want to deal with the difficult, not-so-pleasant memories that this tale was sure to conjure up for her? Was she lingering in Eden to prepare herself for some kind of descent into Hell? But he didn't steer her more quickly to the story he knew was coming. "I have," he told himself, "to be patient. Pushing might not be the best strategy."

Keturah was still talking about Paradise, describing how the four of them would scamper through their Neverland like Peter Pan and the lost boys, playing hide-and-seek and other children's games; climbing trees, picking fruit, laughing and talking and screaming at the top of their voices and enjoying the sounds of Nature as kiskadees, hummingbirds, toucans, semp, parrots and a whole bevy of birds whistled and twittered and sang away in the land.

"It had a river," she said. "Hum… it was running through the estate. We use to have plenty fun bathing in the river during the holidays and playing house in the bamboo patch, a ring ah tall, green bamboo like a big nest with plenty, plenty soft, dry, yellowish- brown bamboo leaf in the centre."

"Must have been beautiful, I'm sure. What spoiled it for you?"

She gave him a look that said she had just returned against her will from some wonderful, far-off world.

"My father," she explained, delivering each word slowly, clearly, "join the new Masjid and decide one day just so, just so that all ah we have to move to town."

She went silent, swallowed, sighed. Ace waited, thinking that this was at last the introduction of the loss of Paradise. "That," she said eventually, barely audibly, "was the first nail in Khalid coffin."

An "Ah! At last!" was in the front of his mind but never reached his tongue as she continued.

"At first, we live Diego, Hill Street, in a lil three-room house."

"Three *bed*rooms," Ace corrected her.

"No, three *rooms*," she repeated. "That asshole of a man leave he good, big, big house in Arma and have mother, father and four children in a three-*room* house! And when my mother complain, he want to beat she up."

Ace put the recorder on pause and got up. "Hold a minute," he said. "You need another drink. As do I," he added quickly to head off her protest, and he headed towards the juice bar.

On his return, he joked, "I have a sense that things starting to heat up, so I put some extra ice. Man beating woman is trouble."

She did not find it amusing. All business. She took one sip of her drink, and he re-started the recording. At first, she explained, her father took her and Khalid to town on Sunday evening and left them all week with a family on the Masjid Compound. He would take them home every Friday after Jumah and they would spend the weekend in Diego Martin. By the mid-to-late eighties, all four of the children were going to school at the Masjid and Khalid was living there full time.

"And the house in Arma?" Ace asked.

"Empty," she replied, her disapproval almost palpable. "Not a soul in it!"

"Town life affect all ah we," she continued. "I could'a see how my brother was changing. He stop laughing, then he stop talking."

"So, the coup attempt did not surprise you?" Ace enquired. "You must have felt something was in the making?"

"Nah!" she responded. "I didn't have a clue. I just know something was eating out my brother guts. But asshole never notice; he was too busy shining the Amir balls."

"So, how *did* you find out about the coup?"

"It was July, remember, school holidays. We was in Arma; we always use to go back Arma for the holidays. But that year Khalid didn't come; he stay down on the Masjid."

"And where was your father?" Ace asked. "He was still a Masjid member, wasn't he?"

"How you mean way he was?" she scoffed. "Way, you think he was? He hardly use to come home. We didn't really miss him until we see him on TV."

The tears welled up in her eyes and she took her glasses off and dried them. Ace thought hers were the saddest eyes he had ever seen.

"You saw him on TV? Doing what?"

"He was on TV with a gun in he hand, standing up behind the Khalif. I bawl."

"Were you worried about what might happen to your father?"

"Doh be stupid!" she shot him down. "I didn't care one ass about he!"

One or two heads around them jerked at her explosive obscenity and an oldish couple with three children, perhaps their grandchildren, sucked their teeth in unison. Ace apologized with a wave of his hand and then signalled to Keturah to tone it down.

Keturah didn't take kindly to the move. "I go talk as loud as I want," she said defiantly before explaining that it was the sight of one of the teenaged boys there behind the Khalif, among the half a dozen armed 'soldiers' posing with him on the TV that had brought home to her the very real and present danger that loomed over her beloved brother. That was when she realized for the first time that Khalid, too, might be somewhere inside the building, might be a 'soldier' involved in the coup.

"That was 1990, remember?" she reminded Ace. "It didn't have no cell phone and WhatsApp and all them thing. Mama and Papa and my mother make a hundred phone calls, but nobody they call didn't know nothing. And strangers answer the phone in the Masjid."

The next day, things got worse when what seemed like the entire Army and Police Force raided her grandmother's home. Her grandfather had a heart attack. She and her siblings were in the mini forest, trying to take their minds off what was happening in Port-of-Spain, in the Red House and Television House, when Ham loudly announce that "The bush moving!" Certain that the daily dose of river water he always had was befogging his brain, she followed the direction of his gaze.

"He say, 'Allyuh, look!' and he get serious, serious. 'The bush moving. No joke. I not lying.' I stop and I tell the other two to stop too. He wasn't lying; the bush was moving in truth."

"I tell them, 'Run!'" And the three ah we take off like a jet in the direction ah Mama house."

But, as she explained, a squad of soldiers who were already there and who marched them into the house with their hands in the air greeted them.

Other soldiers were turning the place upside down. Within minutes, a detachment emerged, obscuring from view her mother and grandmother whom they had encircled.

"Mama didn't fraid them at all," Keturah said. "She was giving them good, back, belly, front, *and* side. Mama was telling them that it have terrorist threatening to kill the entire government, but allyuh cyar find nothing better to do than harass two old people and a woman and some chirren. Allyuh *real* brave."

"Eh, way Papa? I ask Mama when I suddenly realize he wasn't nowhere in the house or in the yard."

Mere moments later, some soldiers brought her grandfather into the house on a stretcher. He was as white as cumulo-nimbus clouds at midday, and his wife was livid.

"'You trying to kill my husband?'" Mama asked, addressing herself to the colonel, who was clearly running the show. "'He's a sick man; his heart simply cannot take this sort of thing!'"

When the soldiers revived her grandfather, he cried uncontrollably. He had been over the river near the animal pen when the troops arrived. Nearly two dozen of them trained their guns on him and ordered him to come with them. They surrounded him and marched him across the bridge with his hands in the air, but he only made it halfway across before he slumped to the ground.

"'If allyuh kill my grandfather,' I tell them, 'allyuh have to frigging well kill me too!'"

"The fellah in charge - was a colonel - say, 'Ah! A young lady with spunk.' I was only sixteen buh me didn't fraid him. I tell him 'Fock you!' And I hawk and spit at him. He say, 'Take her outside and let the fresh air cool her down.'"

"One ah the soldiers who was the spitting image of colonel come and hold my hand and trying to carry me out the house. 'Doh frigging touch me, mister!' I tell him and I pull way my hand. 'Why yuh ent pick on somebody yuh own size?'"

Although she was a Muslim, she wore neither hijab nor jilbab. On this day she dressed in 'home clothes', a pair of three-quarter tights and a shortish jersey, and she wore a full head of long, curly, wild hair which was uncombed and uncovered.

Disregarding her own, her grandmother's and her mother's protests, a pair of soldiers took one arm each, lifted her off her feet and took her out of the house, kicking and screaming and spitting saliva and invectives at them.

An entire group of glum-faced soldiers in battle gear stood in the yard, none of whom appeared entirely pleased with the roles assigned to them in this national crisis. From their animated conversation, Keturah gathered that they would have relished active parts in some of the action taking place in the capital city.

Seated in the back of an army vehicle under the watchful eyes of Lookalike and Helpmate, Keturah felt like a proper prisoner. She shut her eyes tight and tried to think of how to escape; however, every time she opened her eyes, she would find Helpmate looking straight at her. Once, when he thought nobody else was looking, he even fondled himself and mouthed the F-word at her. It made her uneasy. She averted her gaze and refused to look in his direction anymore.

She listened in on the conversations of the soldiers who were still standing around in the yard. That was how she learned that in the Red House the Prime Minister had bravely ordered the troops outside to "Attack with full force!" The military high command had not complied but had opted to let the insurrectionists holed up in the building know just how much firepower they had at their disposal. For the better part of an hour, she discovered, heavy artillery had thundered in the city centre as the Army pounded the Seat of Government with their biggest guns.

"It had forty-something ah them, but only three people didn't survive it," she told Ace. "Three! And one, ah them, was my 18-year-old brother."

"My father," she added, biting off each word and spitting it at Ace, "put a gun in he innocent son hand and put him in the firing line."

"Is always the chirren who does suffer," she continued.

"My brother dead, dead and gone, and my asshole father walk outta it holding a gun over he head and he rest it down and surrender. He ent get a scratch. And my mother went and look for him and carry food and all kinda things for him in the two years he spend in jail."

"And then when some asshole judge let him go, let all ah them go and he come home, he have the gall to hit my mother when she tell him he kill she son. But he make the mistake ah thinking that just because he didn't use to protect she, my mother didn't have nobody else to protect she."

She took the empty paper cup up off the table and crumpled it into a tight ball.

"I never had a father to protect me," she said emphatically. "In fact, we never had a father. He did name father, but he wasn't no real father. He take we brother and let him get kill. For what? Nothing! For Jihad! We had to deal with tusty soldiers for he Jihad!"

The last word coated with contempt so thick it would have made scarcely any noise had it fallen to the floor.

She got to her feet. "That is it," she said, with a shrug, reaching for the recorder. "That is my story."

Ace beat her to it. "No," he protested. "There's more. Whatever happened to your sister and other brother?

And what did you mean by 'tusty soldiers'? What exactly happened?"

She shook her head slowly. Then she took her glasses off and rubbed them with the end of her hijab. Ace thought she had the hard, pitiless, ice green eyes of an assassin.

"You so innocent," she said eventually, putting her glasses back on. "You really don't know what happen? I really must read and spell for you?"

She looked through the sights of an imaginary gun and squeezed an imaginary trigger. Ace froze. There was something about the way she did it that left him in no doubt. The temperature of the Food Court was suddenly wintry. In July. Ace shuddered. Clutching the still whirring tape recorder, his fingers suddenly felt frost bitten.

"Keturah!" he said, without the slightest conviction.

The cry fell on deaf ears. She turned and walked down the eastern stairs, out into Frederick Street and, except for the accompanying letter, she subsequently dropped off at the *ClearCut* office for him, out of his life once and for all.

With a loud click, Ace switched the recorder off.

Tonight, as he waited for the ceremony to start at the Crown Hotel. reaching into his bag, Ace took the letter out of the big brown envelope in which it had come and read it yet another time.

"Dear Ace," it said. "How are you? I trust that you are enjoying the best of health, unearthing tons of gripping stories - and staying off other women's toes!"

"I have given a lot of thought to my little therapeutic session with you, and I have concluded that I am deeply in your debt. For many, many years, this thing has been going on inside of me and I think it was eating away at my entrails. I think it might even be accurate to say that I am a new person since we had our little chat. I feel light, liberated, a significant burden was lifted off my shoulders. That would not have happened if you had not insisted on buying me a drink."

"By the time you read this, I will probably be in Syria, at the very least in Turkey. I have signed on to work with ISIS (surprised, yes, sounds contradictory after our little therapeutic session; but I will do my work against ISIS). Although, I know they won't let me near the frontline; fighting, they have already told me, is man's work. They think women do not have what it takes to kill anyone but themselves. Ha! But you can attest to the fact that they are not the only ones who so delude themselves; you journalists are good at seeing how men truncate lives, but you probably don't perceive, and you certainly don't seem to care how they destroy lives. And you never, *never* imagine that women can and do, sometimes take matters into their own hands, and exact their own vengeance."

How he would have liked to engage her in that, to point out how wrong she was. If he had read the letter a dozen times, a dozen times he bristled at the affront, more than upset, angry, even, that she would say these things to him when he had no chance to defend himself and his profession.

He resumed his reading. "Not all women, of course. My sister's response to being ravaged at so young an age was to give herself to almost any man who was interested. How else do you explain that, at 38, she has eight children—with seven different fathers! I think she would have been better off responding like Ann-Marie, ensuring that she got paid for her efforts."

"Khalid had no chance to make anything of himself once he forcibly entered the Masjid's River."

"Hamidullah disappeared off the face of the Earth and we have not heard from him since. Who can say for certain where he is or what happened to him? Not I. My mother would have allowed her husband to continue to beat her if I had not put an end to it. I'll never forget the look of fear in his eyes when he saw the gun in my hand… I was the one who pulled the trigger, but we were all getting our own back."

Ace couldn't go on. He folded the letter and stuffed it back into the envelope. Then he turned around to look towards the section where his parents sat among the specially invited guests. His father gave him a thumbs up. Ace smiled, saluted, and turned to face the front once more. He shut his eyes tight. Suddenly, he could hear her high-pitched voice once again as she strung the fluent sentences of her terrible tale together, pausing only to catch her breath or to fight back the emotion that occasionally threatened to overwhelm her.

"If things go well, Keturah," he whispered, settling comfortably back in his seat as the house DJ turned the music down and the two presenters made their way onstage, "tonight may well be the biggest night of my life. If it is, it all belongs to you."

"Ladies and gentlemen," Faine Fraser began, "welcome to the 2015 Media Awards Ceremony...."

Days of Armageddon

A big minister woman get shoot; she was the Director ah
Public Persecution. One ah the bigwigs in the
government that was rallying for disbanding The
Compound. She get shoot down coming out ah a casino
one night in December 1989. Four masked men, in full
military gear jump out ah an unmarked black SUV as she
come out. They spray she down, I hear she body was a
strainer after that, only holes.

I don't need to mention where the finger was pointing.
The Khalif had a series ah meeting with some big
officials outside ah court after that to try to 'work it out'
and cool the heat that was mounting. But the dam done
break the bridge. That didn't stop the government in the
Red House from putting up a joint police and soldier
camp at the back ah The Compound.

The Khalif, "not falling for that cock and bull nonsense."
He big team ah lawyers from the Queen's land only

dropping lawsuit after lawsuit on the government, the army chief, and anybody else who The Khalif feel to drop lawsuit on. Everybody in court clothes right through. He want the soldiers and police removed from the land. It went back and forth, court bacchanal and more with The Khalif and the government. The government claim the land was not on The Compound's deed.

The camp was next to we yard; we house was at the back ah The Compound. I used to sit down on a stool by meh bedroom window upstairs and pelt pebbles at the soldiers. I make it bounce on the ground and hit them on their calves. Sometimes, I would see them looking at me after and shaking their head like, 'Nah, she didn't pelt me, I mash a stone, and it pitch up.' I used to smile and wave anytime I see them watching me.

The government lost in the privy court in the Queen's land. The order was to remove the soldiers. They did not follow the order. The Khalif keep up the protest, and things get more out ah hand. Khalif and Abi them was piss. Some soldiers was tracking the women, them brothers was not taking that jusso. Then is police raids like rain in wet season on The Compound. Licks like peas passing in raids. Scar Face they take him down to the station 'for questioning,' he end up dead while in police custody.

The police say, "He tried to attack an officer with an unknown object, which he pulled from his pocket while in custody."

An officer fired at him. Head shot. The object that he had attack them with is still unknown up to today. Not to mention that he was in handcuffs when he 'pulled the object'. That set a darker cloud on The Compound, and it finish fall from there.

On the night ah 8th December 1989, the mood at The Compound get even more dismal. The news 'bout Brother Abdul Kamal, a much-loved member of The Compound, who was also an agricultural teacher and widely known by many. He was a peacemaker and African Cultural icon. While he was in police custody in St. Peters, an individual stabbed him to death. The assailant was unknown.

He even butt head with The Khalif a couple times over things he did not agree with. One thing all Compound members did learn sooner or later was yuh never find yourself butting heads with the Khalif. Let me sidestep here and show allyuh why. Once, a higher up member didn't agree with The Khalif, he challenge he and call for change. One morning, that member was praying in his house. At his front window downstairs, two angels resembling gunmen appeared and offloaded some high-power corn from 'the lord.' He get paralyzed and was in a coma for months. He, he wife and chirren had to *vamanos* from sweet Trinidad.

So, anyway, as I was telling allyuh, Brother Abdul Kamal had gone to St Peters for roti. Apparently, he did not go to the roti shop that he usually went to. Instead, he went to the worst roti shop in the worst street in St Peters. This was surprising given how careful Brother Abdul Kamal was 'bout where he ate and the places he went. He was standing on the pavement on this street when he was "arrested on the charge of suspicion of or loitering" or whatever choice you want to make between these two. The police couldn't make up their mind which one it was.

"We were on patrol in that area. He was looking like he was doing suspicious activities," whatever that was, and as they "were taking him into custody, someone ran up and stabbed him."

Well, don't shoot the messenger, I just say what the police say. Don't ask me how a man run up and stab a next man over twenty-four times while the police with big guns taking the victim into their custody. And the assailant had time to get away, too. Of course, they "pursued the assailant but was unable to apprehend or arrest him or her." They weren't sure if it was a man or woman, either.

The other version ah this tale was that the police saw him on the other street where he usually went for his roti, stop him and he got into the van. An eyewitness said, "he did not refuse. The police spoke to him, he got into their vehicle, and they drove away with him". After this, his demise followed. Anyhow, there was an investigation into the matter, two policemen was charge for kidnapping and or wrongful arrest, and obstruction of justice, but nobody was charge for murder. And none ah them did jail time; the case get throw out under some technicality.

I could still see his body by the Wudu area, getting bathe and wrap for burial. Even the cattle on The Compound mourn the death ah the man who use to take care ah them. As them was washing his body, the cattle come up right in the yard and mooing loud. People trying to run them to the back way they usually was and none ah them moving. I swear there was tears in their eyes. The Compound was a ghost hall after that, and then a storm come and raise the dead.

After the shooting, ah Scar Face and then the death ah Brother Abdul Kamal, The Khalif hold the biggest rally they ever had. The place locked down when they walk through town the day ah brother Abdul Kamal funeral with the body. They do the janaza in The Compound, then drive to town and walk back from town straight to the cemetery that was opposite The Compound.

Plenty cars driving behind them blowing horn, even the cows walking too, man, woman, and chirren in that melee shouting, "Justice for Scar Face and Kamal!" Placards and the whole yard ah embellishments in the melee. Police and soldiers like bumble bee in rose on the streets, but they ent interfering just moving with the procession. When funeral finish man acting like wild animal; brothers throwing talk for the police and some ah them brothers, women and chirren bawling and crying.

The Khalif on a loudspeaker booming out, "Martyrdom is better than oppression!"

Somebody pick up a stone and pelt behind the police and soldiers that line up in the cemetery. Well, bon je, is bacchanal break out; baton and guns come out; licks for so, police and soldier share that day. A whole side ah the brothers get lock up and everybody pass in the madness. Some ah the chirren get lash in the confusion. Tear gas and rubber bullet start to share, too. Some brothers decide is war, so they fight back. Them police and them lockdown the cemetery; they let the women and chirren pass out, and then they deal even more brutal with them brothers.

Khalid, meh brother he tell me, is roasting went on there, after, *oui*, man feel the heat ah hell. And them police was saying, "we done in the cemetery choose a hole." Was 'nough baton, kick, cuff, gun butt, buss head, break teeth, jaw fracture, break ribs and concussion share. Line in the hospital like people going for doubles on Saturday morning. Man, that night The Compound was a hospital in a war zone, yes. A bunch ah badly wounded licking wounds. That was Bloody Friday. But little did we know that the next three Friday to come was The Friday ah all times…

Anyhow, that Friday after Jumu'ah, it was a normal Friday—Friday 27th July 1990; Nobody do nothing different. School was on holiday. We had only come from Arma to go Jumu'ah 'cause we usually spent the holidays with Grandma. Abi used to insist we come for Jumu'ah. Since Grandma was "a kafir and not up to my standards."

After Jumu'ah, we leave for Arma. Khalid and Abi didn't come with we. Abi, say they had the usual meeting before Asr in the Square. So, he let uncle come for we. Well, all yuh know the rest was Fido dancing on TV and then more hell for we. Coup in we craw. I was fifteen back then and I 'member, well…Krik! Krak! Monkey break he back in the old ham sack for a piece ah pommerac.

Coup Time:
Town on Fire

When I study it, the Khalif did over Jumu'ah a little earlier that day, eh. He usually real talk, especially on holidays, that day he start twelve and finish one on the dot. I 'member it well. There wasn't anything special 'bout the khutbah- the usual Friday sermon; Khalif warning 'bout disobeying Allah, thumping the Quran, beating he chest, prancing and rah-rah-ing.

It had no arms or ammunition, no bombs or grenades on display, nothing ah the sort, no sign of what was in the works. Most ah the men get into the handful ah maxis that was on the Compound, going as they normally would to the post-Jumu'ah Friday gathering in the Square. Some ah them going to the Queen's Park Savannah to train for a football match.

Earlier on, one ah the maxis had dropped 'the coach'- Coachie- a two hundred and fifty pound twenty-four-year-old bodybuilder/footballer- to the Savannah with all 'football gears' for the 'training'. So, there he was sitting on a bench with all the bags ah equipment, like any other coach that you may see 'round the Savannah on any given day. The footballers reach 'bout fifteen ah them, just dey kicking, stretching, and doing whatever footballers do in training.

But unknown to us and anybody else, them was waiting to see the signal in the sky further up town: smoke in the city from the bomb that was to be set off in Police Headquarters. The first point ah action was that the police had to be crippled. Then, when the smoke hit the skies, them had to arm up-from the bag that had more 'football gear' and head to their different destinations- all the buildings they take over was close to Queen's Park Savannah.

There was other groups ah them 'round town too, at different locations. In all 'bout 114, men was in the coup.

The next 'tory is 'bout some ah them who was on Charlotte Street looking to head over to the Red House, the parliament building. Earlier on in the day, just before Jumu'ah, they had park a car with guns in it on Charlotte Street. The guns and ammo was in the trunk, of course. So, after Jumu'ah Small Boy and four others jump in a taxi from by the mosque to go to town. Gone up on Charlotte Street, buy something to eat and take up they position in the car. Just some workmen on a Friday evening working on the road. There's nothing strange 'bout that in town.

Next thing is Wee oww! Wee oww!

Well, them thought they was sitting ducks, the police stop right by them car, fly out they jeep and surround the car, tell them jump out and start patting them down, them praying the police ent search the car.

But 'bout fifteen minutes before they had hear the police coming, them did see three fellas running up the road; but them didn't study that. As the police patting them down and telling them 'bout them look like 'some suspect that just rob ah store.' Well boy, meh boy, Small Boy was not just quick on he foot; he was quick with he brain too.

He tell the police "Oh gosh them fellas just pass here running and gone up that side alley up so." Hear he, "Officer I know that alley good, allyuh let we help these officers."

Well, the police fall for the story and antics and looking to take off in hot pursuit ah the real criminals. But that wasn't enough for Small Boy. He hell bent on helping too and the other three follow suit. Well, them help the police ketch the three fellas, who was hiding in a hole Small Boy had know 'bout from he old days. Then, Small Boy walk back to the car, sit down, and looking cool. But they bottom was flapping eh and they heart in they throat.

The man who give me the 'tory say he ask Small Boy why they had to run behind the police and help 'cause the police did believe them. He say Small Boy say he wanted to make sure they wasn't on them still; plus, he had to make sure to get the police away from the loaded car.

Small Boy did know the alley, eh; before he did come to the Compound as a reformed body, he was one ah the best runners in town. He used to drop off and move cocaine and gold for a big boy since he was 'bout nine years; he used to do it on foot. People say he could'a move quicker than sand, he bones was jelly and he coud'a disappear like ghost. He used to live in the Harp, up that same alley the thief them went, with he mother who was a addict and prostitute. The Khalif inherit him when he inherit he boss territory. Small Boy didn't survive to tell the tale though, the coup swallow he up.

Anyhow, back to way I reach in the 'tory. By the time the birds was beginning to find their nests, we reach Arma, was enough play, trying to ketch squirrel, pelt mango and bathing in the river. Country life did nice I tell yuh. Grandma had to spoil the lime by calling we inside.

"When jumbie start to roam, chirren must come inside" she used to say before bad spirit and Douen tote allyuh way 'cross the river."

Well, Mr. T 'bout to start, so we ent mind that Friday.

Eh eh, we run inside jump on the woman's chair; long time that was landing yuh a sweet cutarse; chairs was only for Christmas, guest or foreign people. If yuh put your bottom on a chair was a cut-eye that meant *haul yuh ass from dey*.

Nevertheless, meh brother Ham put on the TV, some advertisement going on. And as Grandma coming to share licks for she chairs, *Bon je*, loud noise like gunshots ring out from the TV. The commercial was cut off and the TV showing grainy with black dots making static noise.

Ham shout out "Aliens landing!"

Black and white long line come up like when TV used to done broadcast at night.

THADAM!

On the screen, wasn't the aliens. Guess who sitting down in a big executive chair like he going to read the news that night? - The Khalif. Standing up next to he, Abi. meh father, on one side and Brother Abdul Bari on the next, both ah them holding big guns and ammo up to them teeth. Khalid and two other young boys in the back, and I know was him because ah the poppy flower pin I did give him earlier that week, he had it pin on he camo jacket and he green eye couldn't hide behind the ninja mask he was wearing. We Great grandfather was a white man from Ireland with green eyes. That is who we get that from.

"Umi!" I call meh mother.

Next on the screen, we was seeing inside the radio station was Brother Timbe flanked by two people. One in ninja mask looking like Sami, meh brother friend, 'cause he was real tall and extra magga. The next one was Brother Karl who join Abi them in the late half ah the Compound days. Everybody well deck out in their army fatigues, not a button out ah place and proudly carrying their guns. The radio station was on the same street as the TV Station, TTT.

Then, the screen shift to the Khalif them in TTT.

"The government has been overthrown," the Khalif was saying. "The country is now under the control of the Islamic Society. Please keep calm. Follow the orders of the revolutionary forces."

The Khalif continue as Umi come into the living room. "I repeat, please keep calm, and follow the orders of the revolutionary forces."

Umi had turn white, she eyes big like saucers, mouth wide open.

They take over four buildings: Ministry of National Security, Red House, TTT building, and the Radio Station. Police Headquarters get blow up, real police and soldier dead. They say was two suicide bombers. I don't know, but Michael Guevera, and Deckie, two ah them boys who we grow up with on the Compound, disappear after the coup. We never know what happen to them.

But the drama was in parliament.

At first, the Minister ah Communication stand up by the podium talking, "Who is your leader?"

He asking the only Opposition MP that was in parliament that day and the rest ah ministers pounding the desks and getting they kicks; giving the opposition MP picong for so. Well, I couldn't believe is so them used to behave like market crab in big parliament.

Rataaattat!

Man, yuh just see them ministers looking 'round confused is like them suddenly lost all ability except to look 'round and watch each other. The minister by the podium start shrinking behind it like a cartoon character. Three-gun man in black, then what look like 'bout twenty more buss through the big wood doors. Two big muscle security standing up on each side ah the doors scatter like dust that a big breeze take. Then like man now start to ketch theyself some get up and walking like duck and crab trying to get away and one or two just sink down in a seat or try to go under a chair.

The men in black move through, bark orders, and tie up ministers.

I hear one saying, "Allyuh get Robbie!" and a next one ah them shouting "Who is allyuh leader now eh? Who?"

He spraying bullets left, right, centre and up in the air like is champagne; but it wasn't raining bubblies. Up to this day everybody does call the one who was mocking the Minister ah Communication 'Mr Who is Your Leader' even on the news after they give him that title, oui.

TV gone blank again and then to the action outside the TV station. Man, if yuh see them Compound boys crawling 'round like real soldier. I see a small man crawling on the roof ah the building just below the TV station. Then he stand up aiming he gun at the real army that was now lining the street.

Next thing, he body cat spraddle off the roof and over the big wall. White and black lines again on the TV.

After the coup, I discover it was Sal; he was thirteen years old.

Intermission done back to the Red House. Was outside on the balcony, the Red House have a balcony going right 'round it on the third floor in a circle- that is the floor they used to keep parliament on. Small Boy shoot across the scene, he on a little cove on the balcony. Me ent know what he was doing dey in the first place, 'cause it had more guns aiming at the Red House than it had water in the Nile. Boyfriend, he fold up heself neat and dey like a sleepy chicken in a nest, he gun resting on he chest. Next thing yuh see, he neck just drop forward and then he body pitch back and fall.

Boodup!

A big splatter ah red spray on the wall that was behind him like Jackson Pollock take a bucket ah he best crimson red and splatter a masterpiece on the wall.

Blank screen again.

News brief time now, "Negotiations are progressing, and the prime minister will soon address the nation," the Khalif informing the world.

The army was demanding that the prime minister be presented, but you know the Khalif. He had to make it like it was his own goodwill gesture.

So, we inside the parliament again. The prime minister was in front ah the room way the podium was on a chair. He looking a little frail and he saying, "My nation stay calm. This would soon be over."

At he side was two men in black and behind them three with guns. The ones that was sitting on the side ah the Prime Minister had no gun with them, well none we could'a see.

Then, jusso, 'Mr Who is Your Leader' everybody know was he 'cause he was the only one that had Allah Hu Akbar painted in red on he chest walking towards the prime minister them.

"Tell the citizens of Trinidad and Tobago that they are now under sharia rule!"

The prime minister looking surprise, like that was not in the rehearsal script. And yuh could see a few ah the other men in black watching around like, 'What?' One ah them who was sitting in one ah the chair at the side ah the prime minister looking like the man in charge.

I feel he was brother Benin, a next senior right hand Compound man. Only he had them big googly glasses and a big head so.

He moving he hand like a producer giving the cut sign and looking like what is this new development.

'Mr. Who is Your Leader' he done throw the script down the toilet and rewrite it. Papayo, he start to shell down the place and shout, "Paradise or Nothing!"

Two ah the hostages who was tie up in the corner them head drop like it get too heavy for them. And 'Mr Who is Your Leader' like he ent care who get bullet now, corn sharing.

Googly glasses throw heself on the prime minister. Somebody from the back decide enough is enough and hit 'Mr Who is Your Leader' one; he head blast open like a watermelon.

But the prime minister done pick up corn and bawl out, "I've been shot! Attack, with full force!" The TV cut again. Mamayo, it was raining heavy lead. It had two big tanks that was line up outside, rocket launcher and guns start to do all the talking now.

On the next side by the Khalif them, they launch a rocket in they curfem too. Man, it was dust in the air, not the regular Queen's Park Savannah dust on a sweet pan night. Town was blazing like a bad day on the Gaza Strip. Dust, fire, smoke, metal, and death.

When I did see meh brother on the screen that first day ah the coup, it was the last time that I would ever see him.

They surrender, the Khalif idea that he used to preach ah martyrdom, paradise and virgins shake out he brain. The man must be gamble that better he get three, four wife and a few concubines in this life here and live, rather than settle for death and virgins. Meh seventeen-year-old brother did not get the chance to walk outta it like meh father and his leader.

Cote ci cote la.

Chronicles of a Compound Child

I was just eight years in 1977. When we was walking home from school, we used to stop just before the hill in Arma village, Gunhill in Palance they call it, the so-called bad boy area, to play hopscotch and cricket with Ann-Marie and she brother David. My mother, Umi, would wet we jacket if she know we went there, but the hopscotch was good. Then we went home to old Miss Pauline, our Nana who use to watch we whenever Umi was not home. Umi was doing some class in Sando, she hardly ever reach home before night. Abi, he was never home; only Allah know what he was doing. I think he was an entrepreneur- I wasn't sure what that mean. When he wasn't working, he was in town with the Khalif them and anyway he wasn't working most days to me. But who cared?

We only had Umi, Grandma, Grandpa and weself. Was four ah we. We was a bunch that stick together; we had few friends. My Grandma uses to call me Fu Pong, them names we can't say these days, eh in allyuh politically correct world, but back then it was ok. That is how meh grandmother them talk, 'cause I look like a Chinee, and meh big sister child, we called her Baby Girl, her name was really Khalila. Meh big sister, Jasmine, she did dead when she make Baby Girl. She was only sixteen, eh.

I was about ten when Baby Girl, my niece, was born. I does still 'member meh big sister Jasmine, she was real pretty and smallie, a good few years older than the rest ah we. Although she looked like the youngest. She was not so bright, a little slow, but real loving. She had a small face, little button nose, real cat eye, long brown plaits down by she bottom and freckles all over she face. I 'member Grandma saying she was a Tinker bell fairy. She used to miss plenty school and stay home and help to cook, sew and thing. Domestication was never my portfolio. I preferred running with the boys. Abi always say, 'Asiah Keturah Al Haqq, why you so harden and unmannerly!'

Long story short, Abi did married Jasmine off to one ah he pardners and when she was 16 years and seven months pregnant, she fall down in 'a domestic affair'. The baby live, but she wasn't so lucky.

My big brother Khalid we use to call him 'White Man' but Abi call him 'Ayatollah Khomeini Shah,' and my second brother he was 'Ham' for short. When Abi was home we use to have to remember to call him by he proper name, no Ham in that house. You would'a swear we was eating ham, the way the man use to get on when we call Hamidullah, Ham.

Grandma had own the most land in Arma, orange field, cocoa, coffee, lemon, lime, mangoes, sapodillas, cayenne, guava, chine tambrand and plenty vegetables. All kind'a flowers, bush, and some farm animals, along with the wild ones like the deer, guana, lappe and gouti. Them hunters used to be chasing the wild animals and Grandma threatening to "take off them hand and foot with meh cutlass, 'cause they only mashing down meh crop."

Croton, anthuriums, jump up and kiss me, ladies ah the night. Bay leaf tree, zebapique and any other herb or spice you could'a think 'bout. Grandma was always making some bush medicine for somebody. Every weekend and holiday we used to spend with Grandma just living it up in the bush like some real forest children.

Grandpa was more fun than Grandma, he use to let we do anything we want. He use to drive a green Benz. Grandma use to work hard in the cocoa field. And Grandpa, he looked after the animals early in the morning before we get up when it was still dark. Them was like chalk and tar; he was short, white with straight hair with a few curls in it and a little on the muscled, broad chest side like a buck. Grandma was like the pitch lake with tack tack head. She had sharp chocolate brown eyes: when she watch you like electricity pass through your veins, eyebrows that look like you use a surgeon scalpel to sculpt it and eyelashes like umbrella shading she eyes. she had a giraffe neck and chin to cut you, like them African queen you see on magazine. All she was missing was a throne.

The bamboo patch was like one ah them big king size bed with the big fancy covering over them, a nice little cocoon, an igloo without the cold. If it had a little drizzle, we didn't even use to get wet in there, fuss the bamboo was thick. But of course, when the rain was pelting down like bullpistle lash we had to run home eh, 'cause then we used to get wet. This was we picnic and treasure spot where we buried all we special stuff. Half the time we didn't 'member what we had buried where, and it was usually the squirrels that dig up we goodies.

When the four ah we moving through we little playground is only wild Tarzan game, climbing trees, picking fruit; making riverside cook, trying to kill birds, ketch guana, gouti, butterflies, or any other critter that walked or crawled on the land or in the river. We imitated the bird sounds like the kiskadees, 'KIS-ka-dee', cornbirds 'Krekrek', toucans 'Groomkk', woodpeckers 'Tchur, tchur, tchur'. Bamboo groan 'creak' when the breeze pass through and now and then crash and splash as an old tree fall or a big alligator jump in the river-according to my cousins from England "Bloody hell, that's a Caiman mate" - but what them did know anyway, they only visited Trinidad once every two years.

It had plenty immortelle and poui tree in the land. Right outside the bedroom window downstairs by Grandma had a real big one. Long time people did fraid them immortelle tree; they say them tree had ghost and spirits, but we use to sneak out in the night to ketcha glimpse ah them spirits. We see none and only mosquito bite we use to ketch. But me and Khalid, we sneak out one time with sheets and leave Jasmine and Ham inside and pelt stones in the window.

Of course, Ham come out to see if it was a UFO. That boy was obsessed with alien and scientific stuff. And we frighten he ass. If allyuh see how he cat spraddle, fall down and bounce he coconut.

Next day, he have to go to school with a big bald patch in he head and plaster. Ham and Jasmine was the opposite ah me and Khalid, just Ham was bright, not slow like Jasmine. Both ah them was quiet, always needing rescuing from people and did not like as much mischief, fight and running 'round as me and Khalid.

Jasmine was a beauty queen. She most times use to leave we and pass in front on the main road, "'cause Grandma say no going in that bush to damage nice skin and get bobo." Khalid and me we didn't care 'bout skin, and we had enough bobo that we look like leopard sometimes.

We use to stop in the bamboo patch, pick mango and try to kill birds with an old sling shot that was always bussing. Ham did never like to kill the birds; he wouldn't kill a fly or a spider either. So, he run through the track up to Grandma house; we could hear him bawling he lungs out, "Grandma, Grandma! Khalid and them killing bird!" Like if we killing people in the bush. The boy was a real tell-tell- baby, and always in a book, the only time he was really happy to be in the bush with we was if he was mixing some concoction.

On weekends, Grandma used to sell in the market; but she always presented herself for our weekend ritual. We went to the spa at Grandma's—a good bush bath, then she drown we in coconut oil and chicken grease. The grease use to keep we hair long and curly and the oil had Khalid skin pink. And I guess it make Ham real bright. And well, Jasmine, it make she more pretty, Grandma use to say.

Grandma use to rub we down and bend we up all how to straighten we nose; we leg and stretch we body. A good dose ah castor oil, shark oil and salts was for all sickness. By Grandma was nice. It was one big upstairs and downstairs concrete house and a old wooden house Umi them grow up in. By the time we born it was just the old house where Grandma use to store all she spices from Grenada; dry she corn fish, put cocoa balls to dry out, make sugar cake, beni ball, red plum in buckets; grind corn for chili bibi and make toolum with molasses from the big rum barrel. She use to carry all this in the market with other things from the field and closer to Christmas she use to start to slaughter and sell the animals too - the pig and duck and chicken from over the river in the pigpens.

Abi use to ketch a fit for Christmas time saying, "My children are Muslims."

He always threatening not to send us there during Christmas holidays. Grandma never take he on, she was one ah the only people that never use to get weak knee when Abi bellow. Is now self she had we baking bread in the outside stone oven, cake, sweetbread, and real ginger beer making. I sure Khalid use to get a little tipsy eh 'cause Grandma use to real let that ginger beer stale and he was dam greedy.

One time we even eat pork. Let me tell allyuh how that happen. That time we did already move from Arma; we come home for holiday and when we reach; we see roast beef on the table. Well, we gone and eat one time, thinking Grandma put out that food for we. Hear nah the juice running down we mouth from that juicy roast; same time Grandpa come inside.

"Oh, God Jesus what allyuh doing? That is pork." I spit it out, but Khalid he feel I ent see him he swallow what was in he mouth quick. And Ham done start to cry ready to run outside wailing like a siren. Grandpa had to grab him quick and hush him up. By the time Abi them come inside we done have everything on the down low. Abi would'a turn we into roast and Umi would'a surely get blame and it would'a be right back home for we.

Yes, good days them was in Arma, except for the days when Abi come home. A day when he home would be like this: the parrots squawking going home, and we in the back house eating, in we yard though not over by Grandma. He did not use to go there much.

Anyway, the 'back house', more like an open, unfinished concrete structure with a roof; it had a few chairs, a hammock; tool shed, plant shed and rest house in one. Abi call family meeting when we finish eat. Khalid, recite he surahs, Ham say he kalimas, Jasmine show Abi how she sew all the buss in he pants them. I fumble through my nighttime dua.

"Razia, you see this girl running wild too much, why she don't know her dua?"

Abi, tan skin, creole, sprawl out his tentacles, stroking his puffy long black beard; broad shoulders and turban wrapped head, a few grains ah he dougla curls escaping he turban. He had a serious but good-looking face though, amber-green eyes -like a mix ah Ham eyes and me and Khalid green eyes-more cat looking, strong jawline and an aquiline nose that the kings and queens of ancient Rome would'a die for.

So, he was saying, "Anyway, I have some good news from in town, the school going to start up and a small apartment gone up, Brother Khalid and his wife Sister Khadija they going to be moving to the Compound. So, I was thinking Keturah and Khalid could stay with them and go to school there, for now, until the other apartments finished, and we move up, too. I will take them to town on weekends and they would stay until Saturday. Second announcement, Jasmine, you doing well, girl. Time for you to get married and Habib ask me for you."

Habib, Abi friend, who use to visit us sometimes when Abi make his occasional appearance, face was like the road coming home from school only potholes and he was old old like Abi. Jasmine use to set up she face every time that old man try to talk to she. The stupid grin on his face- or at least that is what I thought 'bout it. That was he great idea of good news, the man clearly had no inkling of an idea of what good meant.

Umi did not say diddly squat, me Keturah Al Haqq, "'Nooo! Nooo!" And so, our untimely visitation from Abi ended up with me getting a stern warning 'bout my behaviour, Umi getting a slap or two for God alone knows what, Jasmine cringing in her corner, Khalid and Ham on their 'best behaviour' and a cloud of sour dust raising. I tell you Grandma use to say Abi mother never baptize he or give he a good cocoyea broom and bush bath. That is why he have the devil in him.

As soon as the blackbirds was pestering 'round the next morning, "Let's go Khalid, Keturah, ready? Razia oh by Allah, is a good Islamic education they will be getting. What you crying for? woman cut out the dramatics."

My Khalid, that was the first nail in he coffin or must be just being born Abi son he done doom. So off we go, certainly not to the merry-go-round; Abi singing Islamic songs all the way. He was happy like a clown, as if is the amusement park in Disney land we going. I wasn't crying 'cause Khalid he was with me and I don't want licks from Abi. But I really want to cry. What else you expect?

We reach the Compound, take 'bout two hours from Arma to there. It had some jamun trees in the front lining the fence toward the road. An array ah black, red, white, and green flags with Arabic writing danced on the fence, a big driveway and front yard with a basketball ring. Wasn't nothing like home, just a big boring field with a little green and white concrete building in front, "The school," Abi said pointing it out like he was one ah them people who try to sell you things you don't want in a store. And a long walkway away from the school to the left was the mosque and further on, to the back was the apartment building - a half wood, half concrete jail with an outside toilet and bathroom. And the rest was just an open piece ah land with some mangrove trees further on in the back, a dump and beyond that was the highway.

I made it through two months of school before I had a breakdown. Sunday morning Abi is hollering "Keturah, Keturah, time to leave!" Umi is dragging me by my ear and deposits me on the seat next to Khalid.

"I not going there!" out the truck and on the pavement. I was rolling and screaming.

Miss Guevera over the fence peeping, "Popo, what happen?" And if is one thing Abi hated was a scene in front ah the neighbour. He give up.

"Razia take your child inside."

Lucky for me he never come back, at least not to bother with me and school up there.

Weekend when Khalid home I telling him, "When you coming back boy? Like you is a scaredy cat you fraid to tell Abi you want to come back? See how he leave me alone. Last week you miss a real nice lappe. School was over early. We pass in the back to come home and when we nearly reach the gru gru beef patch we hearing something going 'burrh burrh.' Well, you know Ham and Ann-Marie take off in the next direction. Me and David walk up to the patch, and we see it stick in a patch ah picker from the gru gru beef tree. We went by the corner and tell them fellas that does lime on the corner and them went and ketch it. Ham went home and leave me 'cause you know I walk back to see them ketch it. Umi nearly roast meh tail when I reach home."

By, next seven months we move out of Arma Town. Grandma cussing Umi listening, I 'member Grandma was real vex that day we was over by she and Umi tell she we going to live on the Compound with the Khalif and them.

Umi explaining away that it was not so bad, while Grandma use all kinda words I never hear in meh life. She was sounding like the American Indian sending up a war cry, 'Wah eee wah eee'. Umi still talking 'bout the virtues ah the Compound; how they had build some other small apartments but she leave out the part way it still had one toilet and bathroom for everybody. Well, one for men, one for women with a galvanize sheet for a door. But mind you, the Khalif had the biggest apartment with he own toilet. Grandma cuss and cry blood, but what Umi could'a do? "Abi is the man," she say, and we leave same weekend, lock, stock, barrel and toute bagai.

After we move down to the compound it was extending, little apartments, shacks and plenty young boys and men, women too, from all over was joining. Abi and them use to go out and preach, hold rallies, march for all kinda social cause, clean up the town, run anti- drug, anti-prostitution, anti-government and anti-everything campaign.

A normal Friday after Jumah use to look like this: All ah we in the front- yard, brothers chanting and flexing like peacock. The three maxis pull up, all the sign we make in school that morning piling in the maxi: Food for all! No Vat, No Vat, Robbie is a Rat, The Small Man Have to Live!

And time the maxi them full with man, woman and chirren. Driving down in town flags waving out the maxis. "Laillaha illah lah Muhammad dur Rasoolah lah, Subhan Allah, Alhamdulillah, Allah hu Akbar!" carrying the chant and the answer back, pounding the maxi roof. Them times is big maxi in play and boom box with loud loud music. When we pass a maxi, we chant, drowning out their boom box.

Anyway, with all the hype about the Khalif and he team rooting for the poor, helping the downtrodden, hordes ah people coming with this problem or that problem to we little clinic. News people dropping in now and then for an interview with the Khalif. But is always somebody getting in trouble too with the police and politicians not liking the way the Khalif talking and some things he was doing. He was always saying, "I am not a politician; just a man of the people for the people." No matter what, a Muslim always stand up for justice for all and people did not have to be Muslim to come for his help.

The Khalif in he big bungalow, four storeys, equipped with all the trimmings with a sewing-factory to the bottom - the sisters went there to make clothes to sell. Abi had build a three-bedroom upstairs and downstairs in the back a while after too, all the way to the back ah the Compound past the first set ah containers way brothers use to stay coming down a long track. Upstairs was wood and had a balcony and three bedrooms. Downstairs was concrete; as you come in the backdoor was a toilet and bath on the left-hand side, then a little cupboard and storage open space with the step to go upstairs on the right and the kitchen behind the step. After the cupboard space was the living room and dining room, rectangular shape, open space with no walls between. But in Arma town, we had an even fancier house. We house was the second single upstairs and downstairs house on the Compound beside the Khalif own. The next one was a single flat; it was much further up in front, closer to the mosque. And it was not as big as we own either.

But everybody know we house for food. It was one thing Abi believed in feeding people. Some ah them boys was cool; some use to look like real psycho. Others use to only train and when you see them you think is bodybuilders and army GI Joes and everybody trying to get a rank to guard the Khalif or be in with the wazirs and big boys.

I use to bypass the track in front ah them boys' dorm and pass the long way when I by mehself to go up front. One day, Khalid say he waiting for me by the track so I pass there, no Khalid. I start to run and trip right by the container. But Scar Face - muscled like Hulk, one ah the security killer machines ah the Khalif, in the shadow by the container - jump out. Meh heart reach meh mouth but he waiting to make sure I get home safe he saying "K K you oright?" He playing a big Glock in he waist bareback; a big scar from he right ear to he nose bridge and he belly look like meat that a Chinee slaughter. He did get shot and chop up in he stomach before he join the Compound. They had to bring him down there half dead; lucky for him we had a doctor living on the Compound. 'Doc', we called him - he was really a doctor in training. He left the hospital and came with his wife and four children to join the Khalif them. He doubled as a biology teacher in the school.

Anyway, we only get that house for two reasons, well three, because Grandma was only cussing bout "living with them people up there and meh grandchirren only coming home with bobo head from ringworm", whenever we went to visit her. Umi wanted to show Grandma that it wasn't so bad by getting her own house away from everyone else. And the Khalif wanted he right-hand man to look like, feel like and be a man. this meant getting a next wife. Plus, Abi couldn't get a next wife until meh mother did move to "a good place like we had in Arma" at least she demanded that from him. But for me nothing could'a beat we life in Arma.

My father handled all the Compound finances, and bank accounts, final signatory went to him. If I was ever to say that Abi had a good quality, it would be his honesty, when it come to money, loyalty, and people belongings. And he was the Khalif's shadow 'cause ah this.

We break bread with the Khalif, his wives and chirren many times something many other Compound members would'a give a hand and foot for; it was like fine dining in the Holiday Inn or Regency hotel. But mind you, when we go back home right there on the Compound sometimes is salt in mauby if Grandma ent pass a little something for Umi, eh. We had to be contented. Umi was never one to question she husband or bad mouth him, at least most times she didn't.

Mind you on the rare occasions when Umi get a good lick and she really down she use to be eating up sheself and talking to she friend 'bout Abi and the Khalif. Well, I not lying I use to listen. Some ah the best 'tory I hear 'bout at those times was the Khalif business runs and how "Yusuf is either a kunumunu or he know what going on and does help the Khalif eat and wipe mouth like fowl. He going and sit down for hours and wait for the Khalif while he inside 'doing business' by a single woman house. "What he think he doing all that time eh?" she use to say, "talking business, what business he have to talk every two weeks by a woman house. Nobody but he and she in it."

Her friend answer, "hum" with a cuya mouth expression.

All this time, I macoing eh, it didn't have no getting in big people talk them days for we chirren. Well, let me fast forward a bit, one ah these women-the Khalif's 'business partners'- had a child about a year after. And the child was the spitting image ah, guess who? Well, I sure some ah allyuh guess correct, right? Anyhow, enough kuchur, back to business.

And as we say, 'So shall it be as the beginning in the end'; it started as an empty piece ah land and ended as an empty piece ah land. After Abi them grand coup, the soldiers burn down the place. Then it was empty families, empty souls, empty lives, and some who ended up in an exodus to a next empty 'jihad' in foreign lands.

Bam Bam See Am Look Thing!

Things swinging on the Compound, the Khalif and Abi, meh father, them is Lords in they own little world. Well, is more the Khalif is the lord and fellas like Abi them is knights or barons and then the rest ah followers is commoners. Well, allyuh get the picture, right?

Anyhow, Abi finally move we out ah the rat hole upstairs in the Compound apartment block; he finish build he own house in the back. So, my mother, Umi, "cyar complain no more 'bout moving from we big, nice house in south and coming to live in a rat hole."

Well, yuh know they say way man go, woman does follow. So, besides Umi leaving she good place in south, following she man with she jahaji bundle ah chirren to come and live in this godforsaken land in town; hototo gul coming to take shahada now and join the ranks ah Compound wives. Time for Abi to get wifey number two, in line with the Compound fashion. Well, as the wise heads say bam ba yuh go see am with this 'tory.

Abi take he second wife, Sister Rasheeda formerly Mona, and bring she to live with we. Yes, in we house; the one he build for meh mother. He put an extra bedroom downstairs; it was supposed to be a guest room. Well, guess what? I guess Abi know he had other plans. The woman Abi take as he second wife was young, very young, a few years older than me. I was fourteen back then. She claimed to be eighteen, although even if she was eighteen I still ent understand why a big hard back man like Abi want to marry an eighteen-year-old.

Well, some old man always like young chick even now that ent change. He new wife looked older than her age too eh, too much night dew. But since no one had checked her identification card, I couldn't be sure. She and she sister had run into some difficulty where they were living in a house at St. Paul Street in town with some other young girls and a few fellas. One ah the fellas, who was she sister man, end up falling out with the others over some drug thing. He suddenly see God and had come to the Compound seeking rescue and refuge, bringing his girlfriend and she sister in tow. They found accommodation with Sister Wakila, who was an older sister living in one ah the upstairs apartments. She and one or two other families used to take in most ah the women that came. Until they had set up one ah the apartments for new sisters who had nowhere to live.

This is how it used to go for women joining the Compound. It had classes such as sewing, cooking, religion and health- collectively known as the Sisters' Classes, one or two used to join the secondary school with us. We had we own private primary and secondary classes, "So, our children would not get into the madness of that society out there," according to our esteemed Khalif.

And so, our new sisters came to be inducted into the Compound life. Soon, it was time for them to find husbands. So, now, we come back to how Abi get he wifey number two.

Allyuh following me? I know it kind ah confusing the way I talking. But the best part ah the kuchur coming.

So, 'tory around was that one ah them girls have she eyes on Brother Yusuf Sadiq Al Haqq the up-and-coming general ah the Khalif, meh father. They say he was checking out this chick from the corner ah he eyes because he did fraid meh mother.

But up to now I don't know one person who I could say did fraid meh mother. She was so dowdy and quiet; "A complete bobolee when it come to Abi," is not me say so was Grandma, she own mother, ok.

Anyhow, one Saturday after Sisters' Class, Sister Wakila tell meh mother she want to talk to she. Sister Rasheeda, one ah the new women, sticking to Wakila like she dress tail. Well, yuh know I sit down in the corner playing I minding the baby while they talk. But is big people business I really minding oui.

And this Rasheeda girl sitting down with them, eyes down, blushing. Watch me, the baby I was minding couldn't do a better job than she mamayo. If yuh see how them eyes did batting down and she neck draw in like fowl when it sleeping. But let me tell allyuh, coral snake does look pretty and harmless, eh. She was a shorty, thick red girl, big, big breast and real bottom, nice enough face, she eye was big and doe-like.

Anyway, sister Wakila telling Umi how Rasheeda is interested in Abi, and she thought she should come to Umi first as his wife and as an elder sister, showing respect nah. That is what do the trick. Umi feeling like a bite up shilling, watch this young girl who she sure could just wink at Abi, and he go fall; but the girl come to she 'respectfully.'

I let go one steeups, in meh mind though. Even the baby who was in my arms smell that cock and bull 'tory and could ah see wolf in sheep clothes, because he start to bawl for tea at that moment.

Anyway, when the idea of her husband taking a second wife came to her, Razia seemed to welcome it. I was stunned.

"The baby hungry, and I have to go home and cook. Take a note eh Rasheeda, Haqq likes his food fresh and hot; we could talk later and see how things go."

Umi giggling like some seventeen-year-old and I wondering if meh mother done finally lost all she marbles in one game. Must be all the cuff she get in she head from Abi now affecting she.

Well, while we going home, I had to say something even though it might'a get me in hot water for 'minding adults' business'. But like Umi was so taken up in she thinking that I get away from a bouf.

"Umi, she was asking you to get married to Abi, what wrong with she?"

"Oh gosh, the girl is an ok, quiet girl. You just don't like nobody. It's good to help those girls. What yuh go do? Send them back on the streets? And your father will eventually start looking for a wife or the Khalif and them go look for a wife for him, anyway."

It all sounded very magnanimous of her until you understood her ulterior motives for promoting this crazy idea. Although my father was a leader, senior, and founding member of the Compound, many people in the community perceived him as a man who was under his wife's control because he did not have a second wife. And in my mother's opinion, "that is why he behaves so; sometimes because he was feeling stressed and less." The behaviour in question here is the kick and cuff that she used to collect and all the machoistic man is boss, and woman is nought nonsense that he spewed.

Naturally, my mother saw it as her duty to fix this problem; to redeem her husband through the eyes of the gossips. As well as she told me, she wanted him "to feel like a man and not feel pressured as he did not have a next wife," because other brothers poorer than him and in lower rank had two and three wife and, in her words, "this will make him less hostile towards me."

"You too young to understand when you get older, you will see. Sometimes you must sacrifice for betterment," or so Umi said.

So, she tell Abi he should marry the girl. At first, he declined.

"A little too saucy looking for me, not my type."

"Boy you too chupid, that go make you look and feel good. She quiet man and pretty."

Well, me ent really know who was the chupid one here, nah. Abi, for refusing or Umi, for suggesting. Make yuh pick. But Grandma used to say, "If people laying road for agouti to run, hell, it go run?" If I was my father, I guess I would'a run wild too. So, he eventually agreed.

Recognizing that my views didn't count, I dropped the subject with Umi. Anyway, I couldn't push meh luck with getting into big people business again. I would'a surely get the rod of correction from Umi or worse yet from Abi.

Que sera sera, talk done, big wedding everybody smiling. Umi smiling the biggest smile, until she lips ready to buss at the seams. But remember that all skin teeth is not joke eh.

Second wife move in. At first, life was coconut trees swaying in the wind and beaming sunlight. With two wives, Haqq was no longer 'a pussy'. Now, he could call heself *man*. My mother was basking in her role as elder sister-wife, treating Wifey Number Two like a princess. If anybody did ask me, I think it had everything to do with her trying to look all cool and supportive and not at all like the jealous, complaining one. Also, other sisters from the Compound could'a find solace and *a good example* in meh mother accepting, orchestrating, supporting her husband and "taking it like a soldier." this was an accomplishment for her. The men were praising the effort of Sister Razia and letting their wives know to take a page from her book and some ah the women were also patting her on her back. Well, my two-pence is misery like company and some men use whatever they have at hand to control women.

While that cusumay in allyuh head, let me get to the cutarse that girl set me up for 'bout two months after the wedding. Umi get permission to go spend some time in

Arma because Grandma was not so well and according to Abi, "Razia, you finally show some guts and support me instead ah crying for everything, Yuh husband is well pleased with you." I never see Umi mouth broad so in all my life, except at Abi second wedding.

But to me he was *'well pleased'* with his new domestic setup, two women in one house; one to continue doing everything for him; down to running by the door when he come home and taking off he shoe and one to dress up and fan he night fire. And boy the pats on the back from brothers, I swear the man had won a Nobel Prize or something.

He was even pleasant and calm home, "Keturah love come and recite some dua for your Abi; good just a little more attention to remember, ok." And Umi face did not have a swell on it for a whole two months. So, Umi and meh brothers went Arma. I stay with Abi and Wifey Two. Although it was the July holidays, I was doing a little technical class in the school next door, an electrical course.

Plus, Abi, I know he secretly wanted me to stay home too, poor man. After one day of experiencing his new wife's meal. Umi let her cook a Sunday Lunch once-lentil peas suspended in water with floating flecks of Golden Ray Margarine, served with a soup that was allegedly rice, and mushy sorry macaroni salted pie. I fully understood why he would want me to stay.

At age fourteen, I was with the programme. No girl child of Abi's was "going to be lazy and don't know how to take care ah she house and man." Being able to do domestic chores was one way to keep on Abi good side.

On this Friday night, after Umi and them left for Arma, I had everything under control. With house clean and food cook, I was ready for the chicken and chips lime by Sister J. it was in the apartment corridor at the front of the Compound. Well, I come out meh room in meh little fancy dan dan. Rasheeda on the balcony is 'bout that time when the blackbirds looking for they hole. I am super nice to get to go to the frolic in front.

"You ent mind, I going in front for some chicken, you want? If I ent come back time Abi reach just tell him I up front buying chicken, thanks."

"O'right, don't worry, I will tell him I sent you. Bring two pieces for me, nah."

I should'a know, she was all honey and cream. About twenty minutes later, I was in the corridor chatting with the crew and waiting for meh chips.

Abi voice come thundering, he barged into the corridor. "Keturah Al Haqq! How dare you leave my house for hours without permission from anyone?"

The belt going woosh, woosh, as he fly it through the air and Paw! Paw! as it connect to meh behind. Licks sharing like rain; I was so shock and embarrass, I ent saying nothing as he put that cutarse on me in front ah everybody before hauling meh ass back home.

"That will teach you to respect my house, girl. I tired warn you, yuh mother have you so. I go fix that; a woman must be obedient, not no loose cannon. Rasheeda is the woman of my house too eh; never in yuh life again disrespect her. Just walk out ah here like you turning your own key."

I climbing the stairs after meh long walk ah shame and new wifey in the balcony above looking down at me; a vine snake. It was just the beginning of a pattern of deceit which, to me, was to divide our family and turn Abi against us. In her attempt to give Abi a macho reputation among the Compound members, and better her life with him meh mother clearly had no clue about the forces she was unleashing.

Well, all I do after that for the next two weeks was go to class and come straight home, no mosque, nothing. I would'a stay home even longer if I could'a get away with not going to Arabic class and thing. I couldn't get over meh shame and Abi bark at me for the whole time. The two months licks Umi didn't get. He was about to make up for it on me. All he wife doing is acting like she in a five-star hotel ordering thing from me, keeping she fat arse in the bedroom and not she makeshift bedroom that they make downstairs eh, upstairs in Umi them room. All night I hearing she and Abi ruction going on and, in the morning, I like Cinderella Haqq.

Time Umi them come home I was so happy, yes. But bacchanal was now going to start. Soon, Abi was getting back to he old self more than ever. The sneaky little lies of he wifey creeping in and piling up, turning him more towards her and away from meh mother.

"Razia, you jealous, trying to disrupt meh house with yuh evil, ask Allah forgiveness, woman," was the mantra of the days whenever Umi tried to defend herself or her children. Even meh brothers feeling the wrath.

Well, although she turn out to be younger than we thought, she had a real big woman head. How we find out she age, fifteen, is a next tale for some other time- she was not at all the innocent meh mother had assumed her to be.

Anyway, since Umi was only acting up, Abi take Rasheeda by her newfound mother to give Umi a chance to get she self-back together. Rasheeda mother, who was supposed to be dead, turn out to be alive.

According to Rasheeda, "Marme- Miss Mavis- was the woman who grow me up, my actual mother, Susan is dead."

Abi misunderstood. Mind you, we never hear 'bout Miss Mavis before, eh.

Abi never see she mother when he drop she, I was with him. Still on he watch-list, he take me for the ride for 'a father and daughter talk'. About five days after, the same mother, Miss Mavis, show up by we looking for Rasheeda with a whole different story about how she end up on the streets.

"Mister, if you know what good for you let Mona come out yuh house. She is fifteen and own way since she was nine. She always telling people I is not she mother. I swear by Jesus she is meh own flesh and blood."

Abi and some brothers went and find she. The house Abi had dropped she by was the house way she and she sister was living with all ah them fellas before they come to live on the Compound. But she tell Abi that was Miss Mavis house.

The sister Miss Mavis said, was no relative of hers. "They were friends who drop out ah school together, runaway went and live by man and went on a downward spree, until they end up on the Compound." Buju Banton was in town that week, was endless party it had. Meh girl went and free up a bit. Abi beat she; I think it was more because he was shame than any other reason.

After all that Umi telling he to "Let that little girl go back way she come from" and then she tried to frighten him with the authorities.

"What if child welfare come here, eh? Now, we know she is underage."

Of course, Rasheeda done play she self with she little runaway and is wife again, she all sorry and innocent now. "Razia keep harassing me when you not here," was her cry to Abi, "that is why I went to the party, I will never do it again."

Abi done get back sweet on the pumpum; he not giving up he wife.

Plaw! Slap, Umi collect a next gift from Abi.

"Age have nothing to do with it is a mistake. Big woman like you, eh look see what you cause!"

He eat breakfast, get dress, and leave in a huff.

Saturday morning, 'What Umi doing I ask mehself' as me and meh big brother Khalid come home from Quran class. Umi scampering around Rasheeda room like a mouse. We gone upstairs, change we clothes and coming back down to eat, same time the two lovebirds come inside. Abi did take Rasheeda to get some hijab in the Indian bazaar.

Umi in the kitchen, me and Khalid, halfway on the stairs and Ham and the baby upstairs playing.

"As salaam wa alaikum," Abi saying.

"Haqq, this is the end; get she out of here!"

Umi come round the step in the little storeroom section, pot in one hand like a projectile missile and a bundle of some bloody looking clothes swinging from a piece of string. It was looking like when you have a big roll of thread for a cat to play with. Well, we like we in a trance on the step and Abi, like it taking him a few to get he bearings. And as usual wifey all quiet by he side.

"Look! look what I find in she room. The girl working obeah, she trying to tie you."

Then, lo-and-behold, she shake out the bundle and it look like one ah Abi vest that was roll up in a bloody panty or me ent know if it was red paint on it with some bush and smelling stink, stink; worse than one ah them concoction Grandma used to make when we sick.

"I find this stuff in she drawer yes, say something now!"

The projectile missile found its target.

Watang! Clank!

Abi and wifey cat spraddled out the door and we fly back upstairs after we get "Go upstairs now, go!"

In all meh life, I never hear or see meh mother behave like that; it was a different being in the house.

Next thing all we hearing is Clatank! Clang! Bang!

"Get out, get out you devil! Oh God, oh God oohhhhh!"

Khalid was brave he gone downstairs to see what happening and he see Umi was just pelting out stuff from the house. The mattress from Rasheeda room she drag it outside with a bottle of pitch oil and light a fire. Plates, pots, pans, clothes, and anything she could'a move downstairs was outside through the front windows and the door that she had mash up too. The smoke from the fire get thick and black and it was coming closer to the house. Umi still going at a pace and cussing, too. First time in meh whole life I hear meh mother voice raise so hard and saying them kind ah words. She was a bull that the matador wave the red flag to.

Khalid fly back upstairs and me and he looking through the balcony from upstairs. We leave Ham and the baby in meh room. Abi like he so shock, he just outside staring at what Umi doing.

"Obeah! What you do girl audhbillahi min shaytan ir rajim, Allah help me."

Abi grab Rasheeda and start to choke the living daylight outta she.

"Grrr ahh!"

"Tongue hanging out, Rasheeda grab on to he hands but he too strong, she beating up like a fowl, she big eye getting bigger and in two twos she pass out and Abi just let she fall to the ground. Then, Abi just gone running like he possessed, heading for the mangrove. One thing with Abi he didn't fraid nothing eh but mention that word Obeah and he used to get green. He had a brother that did dead from that when they was smaller and he never like no kind ah Obeah talk or thing 'round him.

We thought Abi kill she, we had to get out and do something before the house burn down. Khalid move quick. He run upfront to call some brothers and Umi friend who was living close did done hear the commotion and see the big fire and she come and take we. But she was frightened to go close to Umi, who was still going on a rampage inside, oblivious to anybody and anything. Rasheeda was still out cold in the yard. I bend down to see if she was breathing.

 Umi friend say, "Don't touch she!"

Time Khalid come back, three brothers went in and get Umi they had to hold she down and she was still ranting. Brother Mahmud, we doctor, was on the scene too, he revived Rasheeda with some smelling salt. She look a little bang up and frighten but she was lucky. And he gave Umi some injection that make she get quiet. She was looking like them mad people you see looking through the window in St. James by the madhouse.

The Khalif reach on the scene a few minutes after. If you see the Khalif he and all looking like he turn tootoolbay when he see the happenings. He went inside. Then, I see the broom pushing out the back door and he white thoub following it. Well, yes, look the Khalif sweeping up break glass downstairs. I see some ah the brothers went down in the mangrove to look for Abi. He did not come back.

Next thing we see them coming from the mangrove with Abi. He was unrecognizable, looking like a Pitbull that had escaped and run amuck. With eyes red-rimmed, skin black and caked with stink mangrove mud from head to toe, all he needed was a set of horns and a stick to become a Jab Molasse for carnival.

After that episode was finally the end of Wifey Number Two. The Khalif them pack she out by she mother with a little settlement to help she out and I feel to shut she mouth.

I tell yuh "Bam ba see am left Nowehrians way you find them," Grandma used to say.

Years later, I went to St. Vincent on a brief holiday. There weren't many Muslims. Of course, people wanted to know about the famous Compound in Trinidad and what I think about the next wife thing.

"We hear them Muslim men there like to control and treat women bad." The questions and comments came at me fast and furious. We talked about the 'two wife thing'. Somebody mentioned a woman from Trinidad who had taken up residence on that island. Her story was that she had joined the Compound as a young girl and they gave her to a senior member *against her will* as a concubine. What followed was a tale of woe, beatings, and all kinds of abuse too horrible for your little ear. Some of it, the lesser of the evils mind you, was having to serve the first wife, do all the housework, as well as take-off the husband shoe, kiss and wash he foot when he come home. She fled, afraid they will hunt her down, unfortunate thing and ended up there under the patronage of an old man, ahmm. You want to guess who it was and what was the senior man's name? Hum, look tantana here Lord...

La la le la la laa

The Khalif, Abî and the Compound

High on the list, ah the Khalif demands was, 'Loyalty and honesty'. Meh father Abi, score full marks in both ah these areas and the Khalif often spoke ah, 'Yusuf Sadiq Al Haqq's trustworthiness and loyalty', referring to him as, 'My friend, like Ibrahim was to God'. Sadiq means a friend who is trustworthy, he would say. It is a name, all would agree, that sat easily on meh father's shoulders. I must say though, I agree that no matter what else, Abi was never ever a thief. And if a man tell him his secret, he holding it until he is dead. Ten thousand Tarzan and Hulk couldn't beat that secret out ah him. Call on him today, tomorrow or ten years down the road. He will have your secrets, books, accounts, and money intact, secure, exactly as you gave him.

When the Khalif them start to all over to all ah them other countries, he never leave the country without Abi. Abi was his driver, his key man, his confidant, his everything. One ah the Khalif wife, the second one who was a firebrand, use to say, "If the Khalif fart Yusuf face would 'a be in it, he always up in the Khalif caca hole." When you see the Khalif get she vex she cussing in front ah anybody. I had like her.

Abi was the Khalif, everything man. Watch nah, Abi was so loyal to that man. Imagine he use to come right in the Compound yard on a Sunday with the Khalif after he take him out by the sea for his fresh fish and market and thing. The Khalif never play with his food eh, he use to eat healthily. So anyway, after their Sunday morning run, the Khalif carry home all the markets and thing and then he would take his chirren for a drive before he come back to eat in the evening. All ah we, the Compound chirren playing outside and Abi taking the Khalif and he chirren for Sunday drive and coming back home with them licking ice cream. When they reach back, the Khalif walking out the car with he two hand swinging, or he might have a bunch a flower for his wife them and Abi toting the chirren one by one inside their house. All this time me and meh brothers looking on. I can't 'member one time that Abi ever take we, he own chirren, for ice cream.

I 'member only too well the feast that was laid out for us at The Khalif house. Well, for us to share in. If yuh didn't know where we was, yuh would'a think we was in the presidential suite at some five-star hotel. Big chandelier from halfway 'round the world hanging in their dining room. Yuh could 'a run a marathon in that room if yuh run from one end to the next. Granite counters and natural stone bathrooms. Art from well-known world artists decorating rooms and some ah the best Persian rugs man ever made on the marble floor.

But was a different story in we own house; it had days that all we eating was bake and butter or thing from Umi little garden if Grandma did not send a change for we. Umi was a woman barely use to complain, especially knowing that could 'a set Abi off and she might'a end up with a black eye along with the problem. Sometimes, when Abi come home and Umi ask him 'bout some ah them thing that share he use to just shake he head and say, "Contentment is for those who would go to Jannah." Eh, well look here, I did not mind going to hell a little sometimes, nah.

Like one time, them went and shop in a fancy grocery. The owner was grateful to the Khalif 'cause he get rob going home with a good portion ah money, and the Khalif send his boys to find the people and get back the money for him. So, after that is free grocery. Brother Ahmed and a few others carry their wives and shop; Abi he just come home with one hand swinging and a bag ah sugar and flour in his next hand. Umi ask him 'bout it; Brother Ahmed wife show off all what she get, fancy sausages and the works.

Abi say, "What Allah has for us will reach us. Razia you must stay contented and don't study them women who husband can't control them. We are not beggars."

Well, the next day brother Ahmed come when Abi gone on his usual affairs, driving the Khalif, and he carry Umi to the grocery. Well, is ham, lamb and jam she come back with. But of course, Abi was really vex when he come home and she collect a little rough up; he couldn't get on too dotish though 'cause is Brother Ahmed who come and carry Umi. She didn't ask him to do that. Plus, brother Ahmed was a key Compound man too, especially since he came from the east and Abi admire him. Abi wasn't trying to make bacchanal between he and Brother Ahmed. But Abi use to say, "One thing I don't like about Ahmed is he does not have his wife and children well-disciplined."

Some ah the people who was living on the Compound never even dream a meal or a house like that in their entire life. We had all different people; but most ah the people who come down there was grass roots strugglers, going through a lot ah hardship in they life. Yes, there was a few middle-class families or more well to do. Considering our family as such coming from our own home, having land and a big house, education, and 'good south family background'.

I don't know, from the beginning ah humanity people just do stupid things for all kinds ah reasons, sometimes we understand, sometimes we don't; but it is just that. Look at Adam and Eve, yuh could tell me why they upset them nice living in the garden studying Satan? Can't change that.

As for that man, I call Abi, as far as I could 'a see thinking was not something that was working for him. Or I should say "sensible thinking that was reserve for intelligent people with a good head on their shoulders" as Grandma use to say, "not a pretty intelligent dunce like he."

To be honest, as I got older and study it, he use to do the opposite to what he leader use to do when it come to he family. Thing is the Khalif was a smart man. He would never say in words allyuh don't aspire to live like me; all his doctrine point to living in a state ah subservience and accepting less than better.

But in spite ah the big difference between how the Khalif live and how most ah his followers live, the Compound pick up real people. Well, I giving meh two pence on history and society, some people might think and say differently. Now, the country and climate at the time was just right for the kind ah community the Khalif was building. Them times Black Power movement running through the country, the whole idea ah consciousness, unity, the black man struggle for self-worth and self-sufficiency. Not forgetting religion and religious brotherhood.

In them times, 'the Muslims' was known as the East Indians in the population; the government give them a piece ah land for a cultural and religious place. The Khalif come hopping merrily along. He did come back fresh from studying away, toting a Psychology and Communication double major, top ah he class, degree-six years he had leave Trinidad to study, before that he was a young fresh army man- and he join with the Muslims. Soon enough, 'his radical ideas' and their own was butting heads and locking horns and they try to get him out. Well, he get them out instead; they pull away and leave he on the land.

By then he had already start to rope in other small groups ah people, mainly ah African descent. And one main idea that he was registering was how the East Indian Muslims treating their black brothers, how they did not consider them as, 'real Muslims'. So, the black brothers and others who did not believe in the segregation was pushing for leadership and togetherness within themselves.

So, this, according to our esteemed leader, was the idea ah the Compound along with "To be an example in our society and to live a clean and Islamic life."

The Khalif could 'a make a nursing baby leave the security ah its mother arms and fall right into his own. One thing eh, that man had a knack ah putting the fear ah God, Devil and Man into we, and everybody else, oui.

When he ketch we pitching marbles, he use to ask, "Have you ever seen a game of marbles played at the Olympics? Great men are not made on their knees in the dust."

Well, we done know what coming after that everybody lost their dinkies and big bolos. He clearly hated pitch and would ritually take away our marbles. It was only years later, I pondered, maybe somewhere along the way he had *lost his marbles*.

As a child, I had, we all had - children and adults, develop the habit ah standing at attention whenever we see him strutting through the yard like a peacock and giving him the salaams to ensure he hear us. If I was merely *thinking* something wrong, I would immediately stop. Even adults get tootoolbay when he walk and far less for when he talk, oui. He didn't have to lift a finger; just a look or open his mouth. That is the only way I could understand the nonsense that big man and woman follow him in. Like him or not; he did know how to tie up people like market crab, silver tongue he had, oui. He cuckoo'd in his kingdom and left his dirty work up to his minions that was just waiting like dogs at his foot for a crumb and a good word.

'Member Jones Town Massacre, all ah them people drink the Kool-Aid. The Compound was Jones Town without the Kool-Aid…

One day congotay

Ashes from 1990: A Daughter's Downfall

Here I am, post-coup, back on the Compound after having written my school leaving exams at the secondary school in South to which I had been transferred after July 1990 coup.

I remember the day well when my results came in. I was standing in the Compound yard talking with Brother Mohammed; my father came up and thrust the results slip at me.

"You think this is good enough?"

I looked at the paper. English: Distinction; Spanish, Geography, Principles of Business: Grade Ones and Two; Biology, Chemistry: Grade Three; Maths, Physics: Grade Four.

Without a word, looking straight at my father, I passed the paper to Brother Mohammed.

Seriously? I thought to myself. He's asking me about good enough. He thinks that the whole-coup-bullshit was good enough?

"Yusuf, you not serious, right?" Brother Mohammed said, having had a quick look at the paper. "This real good! You forgetting all the stress them had to go through while we were locked up or what? Especially Maya's children. Khalila had to hold the fort you know."

Presumably, he was referring to all the running around my mother had done for the Compound members who were in prison and those outside.

"Well, alright, alright," my father conceded. "I suppose it's not bad."

I just shook my head, thinking, you serious? The frigging idiot who took his wife and kids from a better life to join this cause and frig up their lives? Well, geez, the Devil must be a saint...

I have since refined that view. The Devil is the Devil.

My father believed he had brought up his children as soldiers, raised them to be strong and to triumph in the face of adversity. Coup or not, he would have been confident of having raised me his daughter, to tough it out. That was his idea of love, and I have no doubt that in his own way he loved us all. Just as the man who beats his wife still loves her. Licks, suffering, abuse, and sacrifice is always tantamount to love, right?

I may not have understood his ideology and his ideas of right or wrong, good, or bad and I may never understand. Maybe he was right to expect better of me.

I thought I had done quite well. Especially, since I went to Government school with Government Security Forces escorting me every day; I was the object of all jokes, 'The terrorist, the one whose father was a coup maker, the one who got pelted with rotten eggs at the term's end.' Fun, fun, fun. When I did the entrance exam for the public school, post-coup, I not only earned myself a place there; I was assigned to Form five-one, the stream for science geeks or 'bright people'. I would later recognize that I really belonged in the Arts given my love for history, literature, writing and foreign languages. In the science stream, I came up against the problem of not having had labs or lab books. I had no foundation in the lab techniques required by the Government school.

In addition, my previous physics teacher, Salim Ubaydah, was always busy with the Compound affairs and so apart from $e=mc^2$ and "for every action, there is an equal and opposite reaction", I really knew nothing about Physics.

Although, he was overwhelmed with non-teaching tasks- such as building the bomb that would later be used to topple the police headquarters- by the time I got to him,

Brother Salim was widely recognized as a brilliant physics teacher whose students achieved a high rate of success.

The Compound school did offer a quality education within the constraints of a limited curriculum. Other members of the teaching staff were Sister Delila who was instrumental in our primary school education, Sister Ashanti, Sister Ameerah, and sister Zaaida.

 I still know what a tributary is and how a spring is formed, thanks to my Geography teacher, Malik. He was exceptional, able to rattle off all manner of things off the top of his head without ever looking into the text. Brother Khan and Brother Amar, my Math teachers, were geniuses. Unfortunately, their wizardry did nothing for me. After two plus two equals four, I was lost.

Khan's brother, Dawud, taught himself Spanish because he had a speech defect. He became a speaker and teacher of the language. Rahim Stuart, a nurse who had left his job at the hospital was my Biology teacher. In Chemistry, I had Sister Amara and, for English Language I had Sister Hafiza.

Another self-taught man who topped his class when he went on to do a degree was Tariq Akbar, my Religious Studies teacher. When we failed to get our Qur'an recitation right, he would put the whole class out in the yard with hands in the air until we could recite the whole thing by heart. Tariq knew precisely what he was doing because this often happened on Friday mornings before Jumu'ah when all the handsome young Compound boys were going about their daily business in the yard. Regrettably, he is now with his maker-disobedience to the Amir was not tolerate As outstanding as some of these members of the Compound were, they all seemed to fall easily into the cult mentality, or so I thought. I do not know or understand enough to say why and how they drank the Kool- Aid...

All of this, I suppose, is why I initially resisted my mother's attempt to send me back to live at Tariq's house. Along with my newfound life of freedom from the entrapments of the Compound, I wanted distance from that life. But I did go back, well, I had no choice my mother put a sweet planass on me, I couldn't sit on my rear for days, dragged me out of our home and sent me packing to correct my behaviours. Well, the old folks say when yuh in good house bad house does call yuh. So, very quickly, I got back into the swing of things. There, I fell in love—or so I thought—with one of the ex-insurgents and eventually married him.

My mother did not blame herself for me getting involved with him, although it was her decision to send me back. I do not blame her either, sometimes I did, but I must face my own perilous decision making. She did not approve of my idea; rebel that I was, I paid her no heed. Rebel or not, I was a fool, in fact I was a big fool. I make no excuse for myself. Stupidity seemed to be the order of the day for me at that time, which probably explains why I would marry the man who I literally never spoke to on the Compound. In fact, before the coup I hated his guts. I considered him a stuck-up, ignorant jackass.

He was married before his marriage to me. His wife, my mother's young friend, pre coup, came to our house regularly, regaling my mother with all the details of her marriage. She just talked and talked, as we Trinis say, 'like she eat parrot bottom'. She was also a kleptomaniac and, in my eyes, a sorry pain in the ass. The klepto part, however, was in everyone's eyes. Even the Amir's secretary at the time, Naila, complained about her stealing pens and pencils from the office.

I hated her husband more because of his wife's complaints about the beatings she got from him. Angry and frustrated by her reports of violence, I would confront my mom and demand to know why her friend didn't "leave that man instead ah only complaining." I couldn't understand then why a woman would stay with a violent man. Instead, of taking control of her

life, she kept coming to us with her complaints, all the while interfering with my stuff. I was so mad!

The game changed during one of the Compound's self-defence camps.

Every time I attended one of these camps, I would tote all my essentials: gear, snacks, pillows, hair supplies, insect repellent, skin cream, everything.

If allyuh could'a see girlfriend, with meh nice figure, Caribbean yellow colour, and cute looking face. I was the world and everything good in it at that time.

Watching me struggle with the load, Tariq would say, "What! Is a beauty store you carrying? Allyuh, let she tote all she bags for she self, eh."

We usually played a jungle-style game of men versus women at these camps in which everyone had to defend themselves. So, at one of those hours when only La Diablesse and soucouyant roamed, a bucket of cold river water would come sailing into the camp and the war would be on. As you ran for your life into the trees you might run straight into a trap. This time, I ran into him. Yes, the violent, by now ex-husband of my mother's friend.

In the surrounding trees, lit only by the lamp that hung from the skies, his camouflage almost blending into the bushes, my eyes caught him. I went straight at him, butting him in his groin, where my head met his height. Surprise! Rambo was on the ground with my four-foot, one hundred pounds frame, dancing a few steps on his private areas.

Well, enemies became friends somehow after our little run-in. Long-time school days, in Trinidad, usually when a boy or girl is constantly teasing you or badmouthing you, or never speaks to you, it was because they liked you - that is what we used to say. So maybe I had liked the man. What can I say, I am just looking for a dumb excuse for my stupidity so read on and never mind my 'dotish' logic.

My mother was not the only one who disapproved of the relationship that I soon began. From what a friend told me, much of the talk in my absence was about me. In front of my face, it was all about trying to convince me to stay clear of him.

It did not work. I fell hard for all his sweet talk, the sorry excuses of why he was who he was before, the assurances that he was a changed man and any other thing you would like to throw in the mix.

So, in 1993, at age eighteen, I became the wife of a man of twenty and five, who was living in Port of Spain, behind the market to be exact, in what we call a 'shanty shack'. It wasn't my idea of the ideal place to settle down and raise a family; I was a stupid, young, naïve girl in love or lust because by then I was also having sex with him. I not going to lie. I tell allyuh, after the initial first few times of pain, it was WOW! Also, I was carrying fruit from his seed by now. So, marriage was my only option- or so I thought. Yes, I am neither afraid nor ashamed to say it. I merrily went headfirst into this calamity of a marriage thinking I could change the world. I was in love and in lust. I was now my own woman, free to run my house, free from the adults who felt they knew more than me about everything. Free! Freedom at last.

Hmmm. If teenagers only knew what awaited them in the adult world, and in all the things that they feel they are missing out on they would 'keep their ass' in their parents' home, go to school and take time. But 'who don't hear does feel'. I did. For years, he joked about the time I had kicked his ass, and how I had nearly kicked off his balls. I really should have kicked them off, if I did, I would not have ended up with three children by the time I was twenty-three. Early in the marriage, I lost my compass and myself. I didn't change the world, but I did change the course of my life. I soon stopped studying completely after settling for some occasional short courses while teaching at the Compound school. By the time my first two children were ready to start school, I was already heavy with my third child and had to face the fact that my chance had passed. I would not change the world.

Still, I was determined not to bring up my children in the 'town life'. My husband and I constantly argued; the marriage was unravelling. He played the ass, stopped going to work, limed a lot and got into trouble with the law. After the police raided our home one day, he turned his anger on me and did the unthinkable.

Plaw!

Enough was enough.

"When you get back home, I will not be here."

He left, I packed my bags, picked up my kids and SAYONARA. Good Riddance!

Did I love him? Yes. But love was not enough for me to throw away my life and, more importantly, my children's lives. He honestly believed that nothing was wrong with his idea of the good life.

To this day, he says to me, "I didn't do anything; you just pick up and leave."

Not surprisingly, his family told everyone who would listen that I thought I was 'too white'. I do not understand why some people assume that only white people would want a better quality of life, an education for themselves and above all for their children.

Well, today, call me white, black, yellow, brown, or red; I have changed the hands on the clock and the world.

Teenaged Coup

At first, she left for a day, then a day or two, then a week, then two weeks, and so it went. There were times when I loved the freedom of not having my mother around; sometimes, I really wanted her with me a little more. I will confess to occasionally resenting her absence. I thought it unfair to me and my brothers and sister. I also began to dislike my father and what I thought he stood for, and I acted out. I rebelled.

I did not want to be the one everyone whispered about, "Look the gul who father them overthrow the government."

Imagine this is the end ah the term, school over, everybody walking down the stretch, a 15-minute walk down to Palo. All the sweet and not so sweet fellas from the government vocational centre in the mix too, the lime pumping going down the stretch, and I was the one who got pelted with garbage

"Way your father and he boys, eh? Call them nah!"

The whole stretch ah school children cracking up getting they jones off ah me. You know us school children can be the wickedest spawn ah the devil when it comes to bullying and prank playing. So, now, I smelling like a dead dog what get lick down and buss open for days on the side ah the road. Man, meh head was messed up, and now I really thinking that the world is against me. And for what, for meh father's rubbish. I used to want to melt into the wall sometimes, studying why it had to be me. Why I couldn't have a normal father like everybody else. At that point I honestly could say I hated the man.

One Friday, after school over early, we decide we going Sando meh cousin, me and a few friends. We know school was going to over early; of course, no one thought it was in our best interest to convey such a bad message to our grandparents — and for those ah us who had them, parents.

Instead, we had a change ah clothes beneath our school clothes ready for 'the unfortunate early dismissal from school' that the principal had announced at the start ah the week.

Night take we in Sando and we ketching we tail to find a car to Palo. Me and meh cousin shaking in we boots, making up all kind'a thing to tell meh grandmother 'bout why we now coming home from school. Well, we decided on the drama act, the play we had to practise for in school and forget to tell she 'bout.

Finally, we get a car that was going Palo, a minivan from meh grandmother them days that the scrap yard had forget to pick up. Man is scramble to get in 'cause is 'bout 50 people waiting for this one transport that could hold 12, 14 max, if yuh leave out the double size woman that was ready to trample a whole herd ah elephant to get in that van. It usually take 'bout two hours, maximum, to get to Palo from Sando, but in that luxurious, sleek, horse-powered vehicle it took 'bout four hours. Well, me and meh cousin, Coo Coo, was cook for sure when we reach home 'cause meh grandmother know that no teacher was sending we home after 10 in the night, no way José. Meh cousin decide we done dead, so she went for the whole hog and gone by she boyfriend when we reach Palo. I was alone, going home to face the music and now have to answer not only for mehself but for meh cousin too. Pressure.

Anyway, I drop off by the Community Centre behind we house, cut through the bush in the back, and sneak in we yard like a proper thief. Lucky for me, when I reach home, meh grandmother done gone in she bed early.

Meh sister tell me, "Ma had a headache and went upstairs since news time and drop to sleep." I praying to every God it have, thinking yes I get away, I could say I reach home 'bout eight and meh play in school story could still stick.

Them days according to meh mother, "You getting real outta hand."

To be honest, I was really doing a few things that I normally did not do. Well, that was things I did not do before the coup, anyway. For me, after the coup was freedom days. I was sixteen allyuh. Oh gosh, don't judge me.

So, meh mother had bring meh uncle who was a little older than me, 'bout twenty, to stay with me and meh siblings while she went and 'play Mary the saviour for all the coup makers'.

He was supposed to 'watch you and make sure you come home early and don't play the fool on the people road liming like some jagabat'.

Well, he was really watching me; I had a scary episode that night after meh big lime. I wasn't frightened to pass through the land at that hour since it had always been our safe space. Jumbie never bother we; soucouyant and douen did fraid we, at least that is what meh siblings and I thought 'cause all the look we used to look for the jumbies meh grandmother used to talk 'bout we never see them. And we always used to camp outside and climb tree at ungodly hours. Sometimes, after twelve midnight we going outside to look for zaboca that fall and going in the outside house to get yam from the storeroom to boil and eat with we zaboca.

Anyway, as I was telling allyuh my A plan was to sneak into the house and get into bed and tell meh story in the morning. What I had not bargained for was the sight ah meh uncle waiting patiently for me in meh bedroom.

Without going into too much detail, let me just say the conversation and interaction that followed was very strange and unnatural. He was not only in meh bedroom but also in meh bed. I was so studying meh good luck that I did not notice him at first. To this day, I wonder what I would have done if... But luckily it remained at the point of 'if". I suppose we all have or know 'bout that one uncle who is a bit iffy.

I ran away after this episode, not mainly due to this; meh mother and I had a little bacchanal the following week when she came home. I had gone out to Borough Day celebrations and did not return home until parrot start to squeak the next morning. After all, it was Borough Day in Point, the biggest party ever in the whole ah South. I had to lime. Naturally, meh mother did not see it that way and so we fell out. Well, I get two planass, and she quarrelled. On top ah that, the gardener who meh grandmother had living in the yard to help she work the yam field see and he was one ah the village maco.

After that, I came up with my ingenious runaway plan. Yes, the one that almost every teenager comes up with, some ah we carry out this plan, some just dream 'bout the day we could get away from parents and adults who always feel they know everything.

I left a note for meh mother saying, 'I feel unwanted and nobody care 'bout me or 'bout what I want'. By the next day, I was back home with some made-up story about where I was. Of course, meh mother found out where I was and did not tell me until much later.

I had found meh way to a friend's house – I can't remember how or why he got left behind, but he was not involved in the coup. He took me to his cousin's house in Cocorite to spend the night while he was out with friends.

He insisted that I 'was not ready for the matters of the adult world', euphemistically speaking. The more important factor might be that he was afraid ah what meh father and the others would say if he allowed me to err. So off he went, leaving a very sour teenaged me and his cousin to ensure I stay put.

The next day, he packed me off back to Palo with his crooked smile, a long talk-like he was meh father- and a warning: "Behave yourself eh, and don't let no man spoil yuh."

Is he serious? I asking mehself. Meh father and them in jail, and you're still studying them? In hindsight I see that even though this said young man and some others had their faults, they were some ah the best men I have ever known.

Regarding my brief misguided flight to freedom, I had no regrets. I had so much pent-up anger, almost hatred, for meh parents. Meh only misgiving was 'bout meh brothers and sisters and what I had put them through. Now, when I look back, I feel sorry for having caused meh mother so much grief. She is meh mother and would never deliberately do anything that would hurt her children. Sometimes parents do make mistakes; they are humans, not God. As an adult and a parent now myself, I have come to recognize this.

After this episode meh mother decided that a visit to meh father was long overdue. For a visit to *Sours*, the name by which meh sister and I now referred to our father, and the other one hundred and three jailed coup brothers, we travelled from South to Chaguaramas. I genuinely missed a lot of them, the younger ones, since they were like meh own brothers. But I was also happy for the freedom their absence in meh life allowed and meh absence from the compound that we lived on before the coup allowed me to enjoy. It was also nice to know the different worlds of South and North Trinidad. Some ah the children from South who was in meh age group had never even left the area. Most ah those who did would have required an adult chaperone, and some only ever went to Sando.

Some ah them looked at me as 'a town gul' but little did they know that I had never really explored town life. My life on the compound was an insulation from the other life outside.

In Chaguaramas, the arrival ah the bus bringing the prisoners to the visiting room was a high-point ah excitement. They were usually chanting and in high spirits, happy to see their loved ones. Sometimes, we would drive down to the barracks where most were kept to wave and call out to them. Two years after they had been set free on the order ah the Appeal Court, some told me they still had meh letters and books, and how our simple acts ah visiting them and driving to the buildings to wave and call their names had sustained and kept them going. A lot ah them received letters and cards from me, me being the budding writer that I was back then. Sometimes, to be honest it was just on the request ah meh mother or father that I wrote, made cards, and sent books to them.

The day the detained men were released from prison was a very happy time for the families and friends of the Compound, having our menfolk at home again.

But not all had made it back home. Antonio, one ah the youngest ah the insurgents, had been lost during the coup when he was trapped and burnt to death at the headquarters of Trinidad and Tobago Television after the army launched a rocket. He was also one ah meh best friends during Compound days; he was 'bout three years older than I was.

I was happy for some ah them, the younger ones, it is true, but I was also unhappy. Acquittal meant that meh father would be free to disapprove ah meh new-found attitudes and lifestyle. More importantly, with his return, I also knew that our life was about to change again.

I was glad that some ah them boys who I thought just caught up in the coup nonsense would have another opportunity to enjoy freedom, but I was not looking forward to getting back into the swing ah things at the Compound. But then, I was just a rebellious teenager. What did I know about what was good for me? Surely the adults knew better…

Côté Ci Côté La

114th Muslimean Memory

After the grand take-over week, it was chaos. The country was in shambles and our lives turned into *Nightmare on Elm Street* in your backyard, Freddy was not in meh dreams anymore. He was right there in meh house. Abi them was locked up. The police and soldiers was out for blood. They turn on the oven on all the people who was lock up family and even on some people who wasn't they friend, family, or foe. And we did not escape...

"Gul I tell yuh this is not no Cinderella and Snow White nah."

Anyway, just when you was thinking things couldn't get worse, papayo things get worse than picker in a gru gru bef patch. Solidiers by grandma like jack spany who get mad when yuh coming home from school and pelt down them nest.

The shadows of the trees moved and the heat was now falling on Jashura's back. And she could hear the ewe bawling for relief; usually, by this time Aunty K would have already milked her. And the two lambs would be frisking about in the kitchen garden waiting for Aunty K to chase them away with a whack from her cocoyea broom. Jashura stretched her body and just as she was about to open her mouth,

Keturah paused the story and exclaimed, "Oh God! Child, meh goat calling, lord meh ent realize we out here so long."

Jashura smiled and shook her head Aunty K insisted on calling the ewe a goat. "I was now about to tell you that."

"Ok, child yes, meh bamsee must be glued to this rocker by now. Bon je help your old aunt up. Let we go and see bout meh chirren."

She stretched out her hands to Jashura who came forward and helped her out the chair. And they strolled hand in hand, each preoccupied with her own thoughts.

"OK Aunty K," Jashura rolled her eyes, "you know I'm not too fond of your child, but I won't ill-treat her," she snickered as they headed to the pen.

Jashura thought that telling her about their lives must have really affected her aunt because she noticed that Aunty K held her hand all the way to the pen.

The lambs started prancing and jumping as usual. Keturah shooed and quarreled with them while Jashura milked the ewe.

And as they walked back to the house Keturah picked up where she had stopped in the family saga.

Anyway, after them soldiers raze through the house and land like a plague of locust and turn the earth upside down. They decide to finish up the day with a good meal.

They had me in the army truck 'cause I did well pepper them earlier on in the house and one ah the big boys had tell them to carry me outside for air. Lookalike and Helpmate was my guards; I tried to be positive and hoped they would leave our house, leave us soon. The answer to that was Helpmate's sickening stares and whisperings about, "I never had some ripe Muslim mangoes before." Lookalike was summoned by the man in charge. He warned Helpmate before he jumped out the jeep, 'Behave yourself eh man you know you.'

Helpmate croaked, 'Me, nah man I cool.'

Then, another one came, he looked like King Kong, he jumped in the driver seat. Then the next one came out with Baby Girl in tow. He was like Doctor Jekyll.

"Or was it Hyde that was the crazy, wicked one?" she asked. Jashura didn't think she had meant for her to answer, so she didn't.

Anyhow, she went on, he put her in the back of the jeep and jumped in with us. Just as he was closing the doors a next one appeared around the corner. He held the door.

'Where allyuh off to, man?' He looked like he belonged in a Disney fantasy rather than in this chaos. He was like a corn-coloured giraffe with large doe-like amber eyes, his movement was fluid and his nose like a chiselled piece of art plastered between his high cheekbones.

King Kong crooned, 'play time Mus, but we all know you don't play 'Muslim Boy' and they all whooped and howled like hungry hyenas except for Mus, who was still standing holding the door.

By this time, I was petrified, Baby Girl whimpered like a sick wet, cold hairless pup as Jekyll ran his filthy paws under her dress.

'You in or what, or you still fasting? he snickered'

Mus looked me straight in the eyes, I saw his pain. He said to me,' I am just as helpless as you are' with those eyes. Hope was gone, my rage was spent.

"Yes, I'm in."

"Whaat!" they all responded.

"Hey, and it's my call now," Mus said, "isn't it? You called last shot, right?" He addressed Helpmate, who had by now dipped his hand into my jersey and was openly fondling my breast.

Jekyll replied, "well the man is right, on the roster is me and Mus," he was now bulging by his pants crotch. "Hop out," he said to Helpmate. "I can't wait anymore," he snarled.

Helpmate reluctantly took his hand from my bosom and jumped out the van, Mus came in. Helpmate mockingly pronounced, "Have fun Mus, she is a feisty one."

Doomsday was sealed, no going back. The doors were closed, and King Kong drove off.

Jashura's heart was restricted by the now seemingly too small place that it held in her body.

Keturah droned on: Jekyll said, 'Drive over the bridge, it have a cocoa house, I scoped it out." The one minute it took to get over the bridge felt like an eternity in hell. But I knew hell was now about to start. I knew Baby Girl could not survive what was going to happen to us. But Mus confused me, I did not read him like this, but here he was with his hand in my jersey, yet still his eyes told me something else.

As we get over the bridge and the jeep had barely stopped. Jekyll threw Baby Girl, who was frantic by now and hollering, over his shoulder and he hopped out, disappearing into the cocoa house with her. He shouted to King Kong, "Don't worry you go get a piece when I done, if it have any remaining."

I shuddered at those words. Crapaud did smoke we pipe for sure now.

Mus jumped out and lifted me out, throwing me over his shoulder too. He told King Kong to take the watch by the bridge "I'll whistle you when we done." I was dangling like a dead gouti from his shoulders. Baby Girl screams vibrated off the trees and everything seemed to scream and tremble as she was caterwauling and wailing in anguish. Even the forest around us bowed in agony with the pangs of her cries. I was sure I could hear all the animals stomping, stampeding, screeching, roaring and panting as they run from that sound. Mus walk a good

distance away and he throw me on the ground and ripped off my jersey, then he told me "Listen I'm not going to rape you, but we have to make it look good. I can't help your sister, I'm sorry", real tears were rolling down his face.

"Just take your pants and underwear off." I was numb as he gently removed my clothes and his clothing, he just covered my body with his. He said, "Scream! Just scream." I could taste his saltiness as he pressed me into the ground. I only wanted Baby Girl to be saved. I went crazy because she never stopped screaming. I pounded Mus back and bellowed like an elephant who had lost its young.

Finally, she stopped… the next time I saw her she was a mangled piece of butchered meat. I did not even recognize her. Maybe surviving was unlucky for her, maybe she was better off dead. When we came out of the forest the colonel was now coming over the bridge, he was furious to say the least, someone ratted on them, but the deed was already done. Baby Girl spent the next three months battling for her life. Her insides were ruptured. Her face was maimed for a lifetime.

She never spoke after that day. She was what you called a true example of the living dead, a zombie.

Everybody ha they own bag ah cocoa to carry.

Raya

It was the hour that the dead man birds' calls could be heard, and she waited to hear the shrill piercing sound of the whistle, an indication of the time to leave. Her grandparents were asleep upstairs; downstairs, with her were her four siblings. The grandparents' son, the revolutionist, was in jail and Mother in the city more on than off in the past two years, taking care of his and his men's needs. But life wasn't always like that…

Life was serene in the countryside of Irie. Mother was always at home, Pa and Ma were usually on the estate across the river and Father? Well, he was never at home; only God knows what he was doing. She thought that he was a construction worker at that time. When he was not on the job, he was in town with the Ismal Party.

Ten-year-old Raya and her siblings walked to and from school with other children from the neighbourhood, kicking crapaud, picking gru gru bef and paddu, ringing the house bells and running off and harassing the dogs and cats along the way. Being the eldest grandchild of the renowned estate owner in the village, she couldn't be as adventurous as the other children, because some maco would see and then Ma would give them a good cutarse when they got home. She always thought that the villagers were telepathic soucouyants. How else could they see, hear, and know everything and report to Ma before the children could even think about doing things? So, after school she did not stray much like the other children, she and her siblings went home and basically played the afternoon away on their grandparents' estate. There was always something to do on the estate- besides the things that Ma wanted them to do that never got done. The estate was like an enchanted forest with acres of flowers like orchids and anthuriums; fields of fruit trees; cocoa and coffee fields; Ma's variety of herbs and spices; massive grooves of bamboo lining the riverbank; teak, palm trees and the majestic towering cypress and silk cotton trees scattered across the land. Nestled inside this forest were her grandparents' two story four-bedroom concrete house and 'the old house' with its large porcelain ancient looking bathtub which she and all her siblings fitted into quite comfortably. This was the two-bedroom wooden house where her father and his nine siblings had grown up.

Some days they had a treasure hunt, other days a picnic, they climbed the pommerac and mango trees, they fished in the river or just fed the caimans- well the argument was always about 'It's an alligator', and the younger ones insisting 'No is crocodile', while 'no, we only have caiman' her older brother Raul, the serious one usually insisted. Sometimes, they caught small river crabs, drain fish, river fish and boiled them in milk pans on the riverbank. They never ate it but whenever their foreign English or Yankee cousins visited, they would usually offer them this traditional delicacy assuring them that they ate this all the time.

Of course, when Ma caught them, they had to help feed the chickens, the ducks, the pigs, grind spices and help to make the fruit preserves from plum, mango, sour cherry or whatever fruit that was in season. And they had to listen to Ma stories about how life was easy for them, how hard it was 'back in the days in Grenada' when Ma was a little girl getting up 'before cock crow' to do all the work on the cocoa estate then walking for miles barefooted through the estate and 'crossing the river' to go to school. Ma would then launch an attack on 'Nowadays children', who she swore were spawns of the devil 'no respect, no manners, Lord Jesus!' Ma would say as she rocked back and forth over whatever odd job she was doing at the time. You couldn't even think about bringing one of those spawns into the estate yard. Ma would say, 'Stick to yourself is four ah allyuh that is enough, and don't ask the neighbour,' who was a good walk away, 'for some salt even. Don't take anything from anybody in school or otherwise; beg water never boil cow skin. All tub sit on dey own bottom. All skin teeth is not a grin' and finally 'forget allyuh father and he Jamaat dotishness.' These were some of Ma's life lessons that she chanted to us on what seemed like an hourly basis.

But let me tell you about Ma, she was a strong woman, wise and proud who worked very hard to achieve all that she had on the little island of Irie, which she had come to at the age of seventeen and worked first as a servant, then she married Pa who came from Grenada a year after her. Pa, on the other hand the product of a mulatto mother and white father, was the typical laid-back womanizer and socialite, but he did his part, Ma kept him in line. Pa couldn't work as long or as hard as Ma, often lamenting about 'the hot sun on my white skin' but the grandkids usually clung to Pa he was 'our salt fish grandpa', who would let us get away with murder. Ma sometimes left the house while they were still dreaming with her cutlass, a flask of coffee and a piece of bake and she came back when they were dragging in from school with a feed bag of yam on her back and another bag on her head with plantain or some other produce from the land.

Ma's significance, sacrifice and strength were only recognized by Raya and her siblings years later, when they were adults and decided to go to the fields on their own. That morning, they prepared themselves well-armed and dressed for the part in all their safety gear for gardening. Well, they came home with one piece of yam about the length of a six-month-old baby's arm and bites from an army of ants and all other insects that they couldn't name. Now, mind you this was after they spent the entire day digging, cutting and even drilling for yam, eddoes and dasheen. The next day they couldn't even get out of bed due to fever and allergies. Her brother Saud looked like a potato that was left in the oven for too long and he had to walk around for the next four days looking like a ghost covered in calamine lotion, since he also suffered from Pa's white skin disease.

Imagine, Ma did all that work on her own and collectively they couldn't achieve what she did single handedly in one day.

The serenity of life in the countryside was broken a few days after Raya's twelfth birthday in August of 1987, when the prodigal son who had begun to spend even more time with the Ismal Party over the past year had finally convinced his wife to leave the estate with her kids for the greater cause in the city. Ma was distraught, "Left him go by heself" she said to Mother. Don't leave here with meh grandchildren to go behind all them mad people." But love prevailed and life went on to teach them a lesson that left a scar on the skin's surface but an open wound beneath that ran deep within the network of blood capillaries and nerve endings in their family.

Life in the big city of Port- de- Irie was very different for Raya and her siblings. For one there was no great expanse of land to frolic in, she and her siblings made do with the downs and jamon trees on the compound and the big drain at the back of the compound with the mangroves that stood at the far southern end. They lived commune style with over forty other families-in an apartment complex on the eastern side. There were two sets of communal bathroom and toilet facilities, surrounded by galvanize for everyone on the compound, except for Yacob himself, who had his own necessities within his large apartment, all for the greater cause.

Mother now followed the prodigal son around and became an active member of the Jamaat, so Raya became the house manager. There was a school and a small grocery on the compound and most times they did not venture outside of the compound yard, Raya and her siblings spent countless days at home alone or just running around the compound with the other children after school, there were some structured activities like a karate class, a baking class for women, an educational class, and a religious class. The compound was life and life was the compound, school was there, everyone was there, and there was an increasing number of bodies passing through.

Over the next three years Ma's voice travelled long and lamenting the condition of her grandchildren whenever they came home for holidays, sometimes with ringworm in their heads, or with bad manners. Raul was getting even more serious and bringing "all kinda stupid book with gun and knife in the place." Ma wanted to know "exactly what was going on up in that place in town." Her lamentations sank in the river and were carried away. And as Ma predicted 'Who doh hear does feel'. The revolution came exactly three years after they had left the countryside. Raul was killed in action and the prodigal son was jailed.

Life moved fifteen-year-old Raya, Mother, and her siblings back to the countryside. This was after they had spent two months in 'a shelter' for the wives and children of the revolutionists. It was like coming into a whole new world again. Life already held challenges for Raya on the brink of womanhood and now it was even more challenging after the bloody revolution. It was not as easy as one might think to make the necessary adjustment into public school and mainstream society, especially with the whole revolutionary thing hanging like a black cloud over her head.

People were curious about her and her family after this episode in their lives. Everyone wanted to know what happened, as if she was in the city toting a gun and killing people, rather than cowering under her bed when the soldiers came and took her family and the other women and children from the compound while her father and his gang were fighting the cause. She just remembers that it was a Friday, like any other Friday. There was the midday religious sermon then most of the men got into some maxis to go to their usual Friday gathering in the square or so she and many others thought. But, by the time 'all jumbie start to prance' as grandma used to say and when the television in the hall was turned on for the usual Friday evening movie on the screen they saw Yacob flanked by two men- one who looked quite a lot like Raul-in army gears with guns and the famous words resonated across the country, "The country is now under siege, please keep calm and follow the orders of our troops. I repeat please keep calm and follow the orders of our troops!" and the rest was history. By nightfall, the army swooped down on the compound firing their guns and loaded them into buses taking them to the shelter. When they were finally released from the shelter, she even had her own police entourage to and from school in the south. Soldiers and police raided her grandma's home constantly and life was chaotic. She often wondered what the point was seeing that Father was already locked away and Raul, her big brother was dead, Pa was a ghost after the revolution and Ma, well she was just Ma.

Anyhow, bit by bit Raya got back into society, made friends, had a boyfriend, wore the latest fashion, and did all the other trivial things teenagers did. But then another challenge reared its head, she and Mother now had varying views and ideas on life, on religion, and the dos and don'ts. Mother practically handed the helm of motherhood to Ma and more so to Raya, to take care of Father and his band of 'for the cause brothers'. Raya's responsibilities were a bit too much for a teenager who just wanted to do normal teenage things like wear jeans, go to a friend's house or a birthday party. Mother disagreed with everything Raya wanted to do; Ma agreed and sometimes disagreed, but was willing to find common ground, since 'She is old enough and if she don't want to be in allyuh thing then leave she.' Mother was not putting up with that so whenever she was around it was 'Do as I say.'

Raya began to resent Mother because she had followed Father to town and he got them into the mess that they had been in, then she brought them back to a world that Raya had been alienated from. Raya saw herself struggling to find her place in this world, and not wanting to be in

Mother's and Father's world and now Mother wanted to control her, while not being there to support her through the struggles.

This new dilemma led Raya to decide, and as she stands on the edge of the darkness clutching her backpack waiting for the whistle, she looks back at her sleeping siblings. She knows that she will miss them dearly but as

Raul always said, 'The wind always blows change', and the shadows of ghosts from the past taunt her as she waits, wiping the tears from her eyes and stepping outside.

What ent meet yuh ent pass yuh

Raya: Waiting for Godfrey

It was that time of the day; you could hear night fall if you cocked your ear. Raya was listening intently, but she was not expecting any call from Mother Nature. Nor did she expect to hear the watery tones of the muezzin, summoning the faithful to the evening prayer. If she was all ears, it was because she was waiting for the final, piercing sound of his whistle to split the surrounding silence. In a moment, she would be out of there, forever turning her back on all that excess, leaving it all behind with never a backward glance.

"With no regrets," she hissed beneath her breath, surprising herself with the violence of her affirmation, "*no* regrets at all! *None!*"

Creak, creak, creak, creak.

It was August 30th, 1991, and the next day would be Independence Day, the 55th anniversary.

"Freedom Day," she said, out loud but barely audibly, "not Independence Day. My Emancipation Day. I gih dem 17 years, more than 17 years, ah my life arready. Deh not getting anodder day."

She summoned a mental image of Godfrey the way he had looked that day a few months before when they had first met. He was tall, athletic, clean-shaven, smiling, handsome, "A young Keith Rowley," she had thought, "but in uniform." Mentally, she undressed him, exposing first his attractive six-pack abs, then what she thought of as his 'front-end loader' before locating him in her mind's eye in the middle of his bed...

She sat alone in the greyness of the porch, rocking to and fro gently in the wicker rocking chair, her thoughts her only companions. She ran her fingers slowly over each of the ten hand-painted, blood-red words adorned the front of the white tee-shirt, which she had carefully selected to wear on this all-important day. 'JULY 1990', it read, 'For all those who paid with their life'."

Her thoughts turned to her current situation. As usual, Mother was in the city, taking care of King La La and his bunch; they didn't do a very good job of that in the State Prison where he had been a guest for the last many years but, as far as Raya was aware, her parents were the only ones who seemed to be surprised by that.

"He shoulda keep he ass home and take care ah he chirren," Ma had said once exasperatedly, when Mother had complained about the treatment he was receiving at the hands of the prison officers. "But no, he have chirren to mind and he want to go and revolute, overthrow government, shoot prime minister, all kinda wrong ting…"

Mother said nothing, her face twitching as she sought to control her anger but not a sound escaping her pursed lips.

"What? He feel he in the Hilton?" Ma went on, she too genuinely angry now. "What the ass he expect? Some kinda five-star hotel treatment? Ham, lamb, *and* jam?"

She sucked her teeth loudly, glared at her daughter-in-law, turned her back theatrically on her and flounced out of the room, her big Bajan bottom reminding us of a burrokeet, her broad Tobagonian nose, counterbalancing it, almost touching the ceiling.

We waited for Mother to respond. In this ongoing war, she often came out on the losing side, unable to offer any logical defense for her blind loyalty to her insurrectionist husband. Second-best was where she would finish again that day.

"Allyuh go outside and play," was all she could find to say, lamely, limply, settling for the soft target of us children in her frustration at having no ammunition to use on the real object of her ire. "Allyuh just getting in people way."

Was that another whistle she had heard? Was he there at last? She listened intently. Nothing. She heard the crackle of a branch in the distance, the chirping of a bird, perhaps a kiskadee, nearby. Nature was talking to her but still no word from Godfrey. Not a peep. Not a plea. Not a prayer. Not yet anyway.

She wondered what would happen if he stood her up, if he changed his mind and never showed up, if he chickened out. He had talked the talk, saying all the right words at just the right moment. He had sworn on his mother's grave that he would do anything she wanted, even become a Muslim.

"I fell in love with a Catholic," she had replied, chuckling, and raising his chin skywards so that their eyes met... "I not sure I could love a Muslim."

He had gone down on his knees and begged her to be his. Forever.

Another fleeting smile flashed across her lips. Forever? What does a teenager know about forever. Forever is tomorrow or the day after that. Only fools and priests looked beyond that. Fools and priests and adults.

Creak, creak, creak, creak.

Tweeeeeeeeeeeeeeeeeeeeet!

That's it! Godfrey's here! I'm outta here!

She got slowly to her feet, suddenly completely calm. He had kept his word. He had come for her.

The rocking chair, as if tired from its evening's exertions, never creaked once after she relieved it of her small burden. She pulled the straps of her sandals up over her heels, tugged at the bottom of the tee-shirt that had gathered in creases under the buttons of her just burgeoning breasts, picked up her backpack, slung it over her shoulder and took a couple of steps in the direction of the door.

Tweeeeet!

She blew a kiss towards the quartet of silhouettes curled up on the couch and on the floor in front of it. Her eyes fell on the framed photographs of her grandfather, in gardening gear and tall rubber boots, and of the stern-faced Yacob, her father resplendent in white, that hung side by side on the wall above them.

She had lingered no more than a moment, but Godfrey was getting impatient.

"Take care, y'all," she mouthed soundlessly.

Four strides covered the distance from the door to the banister and she vaulted nimbly over it. Then, without a backward glance, with no pangs of conscience tearing at her heartstrings, with no thought of what precisely was in store for her, with nothing on her mind except the idea that she was finally going to leave it all behind to be, day after day, night after night, with the man of her dreams, she bolted with the speed and the stretched strides of the legendary Jamaican sprinter towards the towering sapodilla tree where the sound had come from and threw herself into the waiting, outstretched arms of the handsome young soldier with whom she planned to spend the rest of her days or, at least, as much time as Allah or Jesus—or the mindless, resentful Compound hands who would be told she was a 'traitor' - would allow them.

"Happily, ever after," she thought in the moment between the leap and the landing, "begins now.

Long rope for magga goat.

Home Sweet Home: Keturah's Return

"Yuh see this book here, your mother them did love this one. I even read a few ah the stories for meh boys."

Those simple words of memories of life long gone came out of her aunt's throat like Mozart's 'Requiem' symphony and in her eyes, Jashura saw the wreckage of the family's secret.

"Yuh really want to hear the story, eh?"

Keturah, her aunt, raised her hands over her head knotting them, her upper body in an intricate dance, cracking her knuckles, releasing, and stretching her hands out like a bird taking off in flight before it soars to wherever the wind carries it, as she sung her tale, a caged nightingale.

"Well, what I could say, Mus and meh boys them was gone," she shrugged her shoulders, "'Foul play,' is what the police say when they finish investigating the accident.

I wondered and wondered, why, who, how. I was in a real mess for 'bout nine months-plus after the funeral and everything. I lock myself away, hardly eating, not talking; frighten and hiding in every crease and corner I could find. Just taking valium and anything else."

"Mus's mother, Ma, was the one who had come and find me almost dead. She get me out ah meh comatose state. That was a shock, though. Who would'a thought she was the one to bring me back to life? After I get she son and grandchirren kill. I 'member the funeral when she scream at me saying I was 'a bad omen for meh son with yuh Muslimean family.'"

Jashura was now beginning to feel the depth of this buried river. She felt the underground gurgling, churning, and spurting its way along its channel. By now, she had grabbed a cushion and sat on the ground sorting through the books for the sale, while meditating on what this family secret might reveal.

"One day the phone ring, 'Cring! Cring!'"

"It shake me out ah meh usual stupefied state. I did turn off that ringer after Mus them went to the Lord; Ma did turn it on when she come for Papa to call she. But she had gone to town that day. The phone keep on ringing. I did feel tempted to turn off the ringer again; but I answer it. This was the one time I wish I had a fancy phone with caller ID and all the trimmings, but yuh know me even when I was younger, I was never into technology."

"Uh hum," I say as I pick up the receiver. Guess who answer back? Grandma, on meh mother side, I couldn't put down the phone and it was kind ah good to hear she voice, eh."

"Grandma saying, 'Hello!' but I just not answering, then, I say 'Hello, Grandma.'"

"She nearly come through the phone, yes papayo, and she start to cuss in the usual Grandma way 'bout 'so long I trying to talk to yuh gul' and blah blah. I wonder how she get my number, since I never tell she it when I talk to, she, after I leave home. I figure is Ma did call she when I was down and she thought I would'a follow Mus and the boys to the Kingdom ah God."

"Then only when she say, 'Your father find out,' then meh ears really hear. Is like, I snap out ah whatever I was in. I learn from Grandma that Abi find out where I was. He was looking for me since I leave home. He couldn't 'take that disrespect', no sirree, his 'honour' and his 'Deen' was at stake and 'a promise to a brother is for life'. NOBODY could disrespect the grand Wazir ah the Khalif. Especially, not a member ah he own clan, worse yet, a daughter who he had promised to he brethren but she run off with a soldier instead. According to Abi" 'It was better to be dead than to take such a dis.' I had always tried to be careful throughout the years. Grandma didn't know how long he find out. "

"She drop the other bomb that get me going. Abi, say he marrying Baby Girl to Hakim, the same brethren I was promised to, and Umi, meh mother, did stop coming by she with she grandchirren. Abi was threatening to kill Grandma for 'meddling in my family affairs' and is

about a month she ent know what going on. But she did hear Umi say a while before that they going away and so much ISIS talk going on she wondering if is there he want to take them." "She say people was saying 'allegedly' plenty people from by the Khalif them was joining this ISIS."

"I did not know where to start. And all I could'a see was my last sister in this mess, with that monster doing God knows what to she, that is if she didn't half dead already. No, I couldn't let that happen, I already lost Mus them. For the next two weeks, I was just seeing my sister screaming in meh dreams, seeing Mus and meh boys calling me. All meh nightmares and horrors past, present and future was stalking me like jumbie and La Diablesse tracking a man who coming home at hours when only dead walking the earth, drunk and sour to terrorize he family. It was time, I tell myself."

Time for what? Jashura wondered, but she didn't utter a peep.

"Mus army friend, Peter, he come to look for me like a week after meh talk with Grandma. He was looking haggard, too. Mus was like the brother he never had. While we was talking 'bout everything, he was telling me 'bout this group that training in Lebanon, government people from all over the world was also sending troops, United Nations aid and things was really getting hot, plenty countries was trying to stop this ISIS terror reigning through Syria.

"Peter get good word for sure Abi them involved in this ISIS thing in Syria. That kind'a thing was right up the Khalif alley. After they fail coup and years ah trying to make, they own Islamic compound in Trinidad, the ISIS idea was heaven for this lot. But they was moving smart. This time the Khalif wasn't holding any rallies and telling people to join. They didn't want the police heat. So, it was a hush hush movement. But yuh know how it is in Trinidad. Everybody does know everybody's business."

"I plan, I plot, I wake up in blood drenching meh body from head to toe, well sweat but to me it was blood. That went on for two months until it feel like meh brain was split by thunderbolts and meh body on fire. I make up meh mind I was going back, it was three years, and it was time...

The good Lord, he does send Karma to help when yuh need help. Karma; she does stalk people like a wolf hunting for she hungry pups.

"I convince Ma to go home, told her I needed space, I was getting better. I never tell she Grandma had call and I make Grandma swear on she bible to hush she mouth. Ma wasn't so happy, but she leave. Some days after, I finally call home."

"Ham answer, 'As salaam wa alikum.' "

"I nearly didn't recognize meh brother voice; he sound like a big man."

'Wa alayka salaam,' like a hammer hit him in he head when he hear meh voice."

"'K, K...' his voice going down two or three octaves."

"'Yes, is me Ham,' I say."

"I ask him 'Where Abi?'"

"'He not here.'"

Good, I thought. I breathed in relief. Now I could get info.

"'Yuh good? Baby Girl good?'"

"'Yes,' he say."

"Abi ent marry she off to nobody, right?"

"'No, well... not yet.'"

"Ham was always a terrible liar, so I know Baby Girl was facing this monster right now."
"'Ham!' I barked into the phone."

"'Ok, ok Abi marry she to Hakim last week,' he stumbled on 'because we travelling, we going to move.'"

"'Move where?'"

"'We going away,' I needed bat ears to hear him good."

"'Abi reach…,' His voice, already low pitch, was now quivering."

"I hear the booming 'As salaam wa alikum,' ah Abi voice over the phone, then the line went dead. Beeeep… I really couldn't say who hang up first between me and Ham."

"I had jump when I hear Abi's voice over the line. After so long the man could still make me jump. But I tell myself don't worry, one day yuh go make he jump out he pants, yuh have balls too Asiah Keturah Al-Haqq. Your sister, husband and sons didn't die for nothing, and yuh not letting your brother and last sister and your chupid mother, the only family you have now suffer anymore. I had to fix this now…

The bleating of the sheep in the pens outside disturbed the air.

"Oh gosh," Keturah jumped, "let me go see what meh chirren need just now jumbie go start walking road and yuh know I ent want to be outside that timing."

"Ok," Jashura croaked.

Somehow Jashura thought about the puff adder that she was just looking at in one book. A reptile that bore patience and suffered the abuse of its attackers before it struck and unleashed its deadly venom.

Trouble make monkey eat pepper

ISIS Trînís

They rape man, woman, and child, cut man head, hand, and foot off and put them on stake, celebrated and danced through the remnant ah broken villages. Even their own people, they dealt with dread for infractions or, worse yet, for deserting. The only thing Islamic 'bout ISIS was the 'Allahu Akbar' they used to shout, *oui*!

Abi, my father, being who he was, Syria was the land ah glory for him and his leader, the Khalif, who years ago had hoppity scotched along with his Compound dwellers leading the grand coup in Trinidad. I guess getting away from cutthroat with the Queen's amnesty didn't put a dent in their spirits.

So anyway, after I run away from Abi them in Syria, I had found my calling, a counter ISIS group which I joined. I keep track ah Abi them in all the war bacchanal. Sometimes, they move from a village a few days before we reach; sometimes, I lost them for two weeks or months. Plenty ah times when ISIS lose a village they run for the hills or move to a next one ah their strongholds. Sometimes, we capture some ah them. Once I come across a family that I had known from the Compound days in Trinidad. But I make sure them ent see me. And so, for 'bout a year and a half, I was chasing ghost in Syria.

Until, one day congotay, we finally was going on the mission I was hoping for. I pray to the Almighty that they didn't move before we reach. We had to rescue a village with some soldiers from the joint Syrian and Kurdish Forces. It was to be easy 'cause we agents on the inside set it up; we was marking this village for some months, even before Abi them reach dey. This was a major stronghold; it wasn't a big place. A key spot for movement between other hotspots, as well as one ah the places they kept supplies and stuff, basically a home for ISIS. And we learn the habits and movement for a while before we make a move on them. It was 'bout a good two months before we strike.

It was a tough three hours over the hills that separate the village from the main traffic way. But meh mind was on meh own plans; so, the rough terrain was no bother for me. By fair or force, I was a guerrilla fighter and Karma was lighting the fire under meh foot.

We arrive in the dead ah night, when spirits and ghosts prowling. Guards are running around, but not women and children out at that hour. I take up meh position and wait, the tear gas signal went off and then it was action time; swift and clean, a few casualties was expected but not much, since we had the inside scoop. I was still holding meh post along with the eight other outpost guards; we just had to hold the outer perimeters, look out for unexpected visitors, and just step in to deal with any disgruntled man or woman lurking in the background—some women could'a handle a mean AK, eh.

Everything went smoothly, and we was ready to come out ah the wood works. I was up in a tree. It had a clump ah trees just at the start ah the village; like a mirage, it look like there was nothing behind those trees. Plus, it was in one ah the lucky part ah the desert that had an oasis. The trees make a burly knot ah green and brown covering over the ground. Shortish trees, but with thick trunks 'bout nine feet so average. The one I was in had a hollow out like middle and the branches sprawl out 'round it.

Picture this, ah we girl in she jungle green and desert brown camo, a monkey suit style, black skull cap covering meh face too with meh eyes peeking out, a belt ah ammo strap over meh shoulder and one 'round meh waist for good measure. Binoculars with night vision 'round meh neck. Meh AR was ready to rattle, two knives strap in meh boots and two in meh waist. Meh heart on fire, too. Ignited by fury, it nearly turn to ashes. But I had to throw ice water on fury until it was time to unleash Karma.

I see Hakim, meh brother-in-law who had sent meh sister to paradise, Abi and two other men. They get away somehow from capture and was sneaking out heading towards the trees. Them have branch on them and well camouflage looking like part ah the ground if yuh ent really looking.

Karma latch onto her prey. THUMP! THUMP! I was sure that the sound ah meh heart was echoing throughout the village. Them reach close to the groove ah trees, crawling. Chirrup, a faint whistle: low and behold, a bunker door open in the ground just in front ah them, an underground tunnel. The first two slip in, then some soldiers from we mission pass by. Magic doors close back and the next two freeze, blending into the thick tree trunk in the undergrowth. Abi and Hakim was right dey, directly under meh tree. If I stretch meh hand from where I was in the canopy I sure I could'a almost touch them.

Meh lost family swimming in meh head, blood gushing through a river.

After the soldiers pass Hakim, he was in front. The gun- a handgun- he was holding as he crawl slipping from his grasp. All I had see in Abi hand was a Rambo knife.

"Abi," I whisper, the wind get chilly as it carry meh voice to him, the leaves shudder and shiver. Relief, confusion, then dread, walk across his face. He saw me. By the time he process what was going to happen, it done happen.

Karma spring, I hear the "K" rolling off meh father lips. His mouth remain open and the bullet that rip through his voice box take care ah the rest ah meh name. Meh body sag in its victory.

I slither down the tree. Two crumple heaps ah dust at meh feet, they disrupt and disrespect life and everything that it meant for me and left me without kith or kin.

Nobody, besides the few people who was involve with me did know 'bout me and joining the secret anti ISIS group. Normal *maco* thing with Trini people when I come back from Syria. All I say to some, "Abi get bomb up in Raqqa." Muslim shushuing 'bout who went, who dead over dey, who get to come home.

Well, what I could say 'bout what I do, I was wrong, maybe, I was right, maybe; it all depends on what your take is in the 'tory. I want to apologize; I want to feel bad for what I do, but I go be a damn liar if I do. So, this is the testimony ah Asiah Keturah Al Haqq, Compound dweller. Allyuh, as me boy the Lord Kitchener, say, 'When I dead bury meh clothes and I don't want nobody to cry *coco mena* tears for me.'

All unfair game does tun 'round

PRETTY SUE

A Folklore Story

"Crick?"

"Crack!"

Ah love mih granny; she is all Ah have and without she, Ah don't know where Ah woulda be. Ah mighta be ketching mih ass like some ah the brothers Ah does lime with, Charlo, Dawg, Big Toe, Beak, Bulb, Fisheye and Dew or even worse Ah mighta end up kicking the bucket early o' clock.

Is me and them self and a few other brothers who was coming home late one night from the big hill after the blocko in Siparia. We walking, eh, P2. We could'a take a PH but lime cyar done. The blocko was really good and we spirit high so we laughing and talking; nobody eh want to spoil the vibe.

Fatigue passing fuh so and man files bussing. Big Toe remind Bulb 'bout the time when he wasn't wukking, and he did come by him in the tyre shop to ask him if he could vulcanise a durex fuh him 'cause he didn't have no money to buy a fresh one.

"Blasted cheapskate!" Big Toe howled, " I gih him a pack ah Easy Rider and tell him doh come back in the shop."

Bulb let the laughter die down before he hit back with the one 'bout the time when Big Toe ask him fuh fifty cents borrow to buy lunch.

"Fifty cents?" Charlo ask, "What lunch yuh coulda buy with fifty cents?"

"I mihself wanted to know," Bulb say, "That is why I gih him a dollar. Well, the man buy two suck-a-bag and empty them in a cup. And then he buy eight loose Crix and a small pack with four Ovaltine sweet biscuit. He put one Ovaltine between two Crix and he make four sandwich. Lunch, oui!"

Man laugh like if laughing going outta style. But the best one was when Dawg tell Fisheye something 'bout he Dracula gal and Fisheye hit back with something 'bout how he gal better-looking than he whoring sister.

"Ah swear Ah rather have a sister who is a whore," Dawg tell him, putting he hand on he heart, "than be a trust fock child like you and your sister."

Well, brother, we did done pass Railway Road already but I feel everybody who was still up on the hill hear the explosion ah laughter that cause. A 'trust fock child!'

Woi! Mamayo! Up to the time I leave de group who living higher up the road and me and Dawg walk in Doctor Murray Road by weself, we eh hear another peep outta Fisheye.

From the time Ah reach home and open the gate, Ah see the light go on; Ah know Granny waiting up fuh mih.

She in the join room. "It late, Sonson. Way yuh now coming from?"

"From the blocko, Granny. Yuh tell mih come home before fo'daymorning and, look, is only a little after midnight and Ah reach."

Who yuh was with?"

"Was bout twelve ah we. Was me, Beak, Big Toe, Bulb, Fisheye, Dawg, Breeze, and a few others."

"Allyuh get a drop or allyuh walk?"

"We walk. Too besides, twelve is too much fuh one car and we didn't want to mash up the lime."

"And allyuh pass over the river bridge?"

"No, Granny. But what is this thing allyuh have with the bridge? Them boy and them make we walk a extra twenty minutes passing the long way talking bout the lady, the lady."

They right the lady go ketch allyuh if allyuh pass there late."

"Lady, Granny?" Ah ask she, "what lady? Look how Ah trembling. Ah fraid too bad!"

"Heh heh heh," she giggle, getting the joke. "Alright, Mr Braver Danger, alright. One day Ah go tell yuh the story, one day, one day, congotay."

"Hear mih, old lady. Nothing you tell me 'bout no lady could stop me from enjoying myself. Ah not going and dreevay bout the place to be coming home no late, late hour fuh spite. But if Ah have to stay out late, Ah staying out late and sometimes Ah might even stay out late to meet a lady. Is only threescore and ten the Bible promise every man and Ah want to enjoy my full quota."

"Sit down, Sonson. Leh mih tell yuh why Ah does cyar sleep when yuh outta the house late."

One time, Ah realise tonight is the one day, one day, congotay. So, Ah sit down. Granny mouth open and the tory jump out…

"Old Ma Charles daughter was pretty fuh so, the prettiest thing any man ever see. But she mother was just the opposite, a ugly, old dry-up witch, who doh like people and who people doh like. People like she daughter, uhum. Especially man. When Sue walk down the road is like a bolt ah lightning hit all them man on the block. She use to whizz past like if she foot and them not even touching the ground. It ent have no breeze but she long, curly, black hair blowing in the wind, she waist moving from side to side like Sparrow or Nello or one ah them rude boy calypsonian. She skin shining like a ripe, ripe pommecythere and she lip and them red like a cherry. She plump young breast full like two juicy melon and she two-eye green like the Quinam bandan, telling yuh come, come, like a nice cool river pool on a real hot day. People use to say she look like one ah them models in them fancy magazine that come from America.

"Man could watch but they know they cyar touch; Ma Charles done fix that. Yuh touch or try to touch and everybody know what go happen. The spell go fall on yuh. Yuh go get sick, yuh go cyar eat, yuh go dry up, yuh might even dead. Plenty man from the village try, plenty man from the village fail. Some ah them end up in the cemetery. Almost every man that watch, lust and call she 'doux-doux', crapaud smoke he pipe."

Ah listening, eh; Ah doh want to interrupt but Ah wondering way this story going. Ah find she coulda wait until Ah get up tomorrow and tell me the story then. But she done decide tonight is the best time fuh she, she telling me the story tonight, striking while the iron hot…

"So," she continue, "Sue pretty, pretty, but she lonely; she only use to talk to she mother and one or two other people."

"Ma Charles was old…and bitter. The talk in town was that how Massa son did rape she and get she pregnant.

That is how Pretty Sue born. He think he get way but Ma Charles went down by the river and do she thing with the obeah man, Miss Marta husband. Massa loss he son. Just so, he drop down dead. But he was only the first one. Some more well follow he."

"What yuh mean? They dead?"

"Dead like a nit. And is some young fellas too. Not old man, who yuh expect to get heart attack and stroke and them kinda thing."

"Is to hear them old maid talk bout she in the market. "That zansepree," yuh use to hear them saying, "she make meh son dry up." But nobody name woman enough to tell she nothing to she face. When Ma Charles pass close to them, everybody bowing and scraping and saying, "Morning, macommere." They fraid she power real bad. Some ah them even use she power but yuh had to be lucky to find out. But everybody know 'bout Miss Ann; she was like them man macafourchette, nine children with seven different father. She tuntun turn up; it cyar hold no man. But Harold, the last two father, like Ma Charles tie he up for good. Is only a Ma Charles miracle way coulda do that fuh she."

"Way! Ah just walking with Fisheye, Selwyn, Miss Ann grandson or she great-grandson, Ah think. Me eh know is all that commesse it have round he family."

"Well, time pass and Sue get prettier and prettier. Then, one day, young Evans come back home. Evans grow up with he mother sister in town. But when Miss Marta sister dead, he didn't have nobody to mind him and Miss Marta bring him back home. Young Evans mamaguy all them woman in the village, young, old and in-between with he niceboy face and he town ways. He turn plenty ah them head. And then one day he meet Pretty Sue. All hell break loose. Ma Charles obeah didn't wuk on he. People say, 'he mount'. He father make a lock for him when he was a baby and he lock plenty stronger than Ma Charles magic."

"What foolishness is that 'bout mount? Mount mih foot! When God ready fuh yuh tail, Granny, yuh could be Mount Everest, yuh still gone. Man, to hang cyar drown."

"Boy, hum, Sonson, bonje!" Granny warn mih, "Yuh young. Yuh young and yuh wrong! Wait. Leh mih finish mih story. So what yuh think happen? Evans talk to Pretty Sue and nothing eh happen to he. Once. Twice. Nothing. Three times. A dozen times. Nothing. They get thick like thief. Still nothing."

"Man gihing Evans picong fuh so. 'Boy, boy, leave dat gal alone; yuh playing with fire. Fredo thought he had magic too; nineteen and he done six foot under, dead and bury!' And Fredo wasn't the only one."

"Fredo? The world really small, yes. I think Fredo was Charlo uncle or he great-uncle. He always talking about how obeah kill one ah he uncle, how pus was running outta he head like how snat does come outta people nose. That was before he born but everybody in he family does be talking bout it, he say."

"Yep, is true, is not a secret. Anyway, Evans ent take them on. He and Sue just get tighter and tighter until one day he and she move in to Miss Marta shack on the hill. Papayo! Ma Charles breathing fire and brimstone. When Sue belly swell, well, Ma Charles couldn't take it no more. She decide she have to do something 'bout that and she go do fuh Evans. That was the only time people ever see Ma Charles smiling. It was just a force-ripe smile, eh, a skin teeth, not a real grin."

"Time pass and child ready to born. Who yuh think gone to play midwife? Ma Charles, oui! When Evans come home from wuk, Ma Charles tell him the child born dead. What really happen is that the poison take she and she stifle the baby with a pillow and throw it in the river. Evans gone mad, stark, staring mad. One time. He gone St Ann's and Pretty Sue gone back home by she mother to get better. That ent wuk. Sue sheself loss she mind. Every day she going walking to look fuh she baby. One day she went down by the river and just so just so, she get a vision ah what she mother did do. She get in a rage, run amok, kill the old lady and then hang sheself on the big silk cotton tree down by the river bridge...

"From that day on, people say, when you coming up the hill and crossing the bridge in the night, yuh have to look out for the lady."

Steuppsing. Ah say, "Ah never see no lady. "Ah tired pass on the bridge in the night plenty time."

"Yes, but what time? After midnight?"

"Well, no. But..."

"Ahahn!" Granny exclaim. "That is the thing self. It have a time fuh everything. People say she does come down from the silk cotton tree after midnight, screaming and tearing out she hair and pointing down by the river. They say sometimes she does just be standing up on the bridge, holding she two hand in a cup in front ah she and rocking back and forth and singing, 'Dodo, petit popo' like if is a baby she putting to sleep."

"People say a few man—man, eh, not woman! - that was unlucky enough to see she end up diving in the river to help she look for she baby. None ah them ever come back out. Not one. Pretty Sue trap them with she sad face and she crocodile tears. They say she take they soul to keep fuh she baby."

Ah say, "Oh gosh granny," as I yawn and stretch, "yuh still believe in all them long time thing, not me nah. Ah ent saying it ent have obeah, but them spirit thing man Ah have to see to believe yes."

"Boy go get yuh rest now but Ah telling yuh, yuh go learn the hard way go long man, go long." Granny warn mih pointing and shaking she finger at mih. "Then you go remember and say mih granny did tell mih, oright. Let mih put this old bag a bones to rest good night Sonson," she say as she walk away mumbling about 'youths nowadays.'"

Well, the next weekend, me and mih boy Dawg plan a night out, them rest ah fellas went on a hunt. It happen so that Ah was feeling real sick that Saturday and when he pass, Ah say Ah ent going. Now, Dawg, he tusty for so, cyar give up a pumpum, always chasing a skirt like a cat chasing string. Especially, if is a pretty one and the sisters we was to meet that night. Hum, if Ah tell allyuh, sweeter than Julie.

So, when I tell him leh we go Sunday instead he talking bout, "Nah! Nah! Keisha ripe boy, ready for the picking. That is you; Ah might even get both a them."

"Oright, pardner, fix your mix," Ah tell him. "Ah cyar make."

Well, Dawg being a 'Dawg.' He end up going by heself.

The next day is big thing in the village, Dawg missing nobody ent see he all day Sunday, and he mother say he never come home Saturday night. Harricharran, the PH driver say he did go on a airport run, and he had pass Dawg walking towards the river bridge 'bout round one

Sunday morning. He say that he had stop for him, but Dawg tell him is just a short walk from the bridge to home. The next thing Ah know is black Ah wearing and the church choir singing:

It don't matter, where you bury me
I'll be home and I'll be free...

Crick? Crack! Monkey break he back for a piece of pommerac in the old ham sack.

Rahim and Papa Bois

A Folklore Tale

Suddenly, Savi pushed Rahim violently away from her.

"Whaaaat?"

Staggering and falling on his bottom, the flowers he was now going to present to her scattered on the floor.

Rahim looked at his brother, who had been standing behind Savi, waiting his turn to say welcome home.

"Savi?"

The question seemed to bring her out of a trance.

As he got unsteadily to his feet, she flung herself into his arms once more.

Meanwhile, in the next village, an hour away, James could not believe, he walked back for one last goodbye. As he entered the La Pre cemetery gates, he was almost sure that he saw two figures in the distance bending over his wife's grave. By the time he approached the grave, the last remaining filter of sanity in his mind left. Scattered wreaths greeted him. Maybe the wind had scattered the wreaths. What am I doing in the cemetery at night? My mind is playing tricks. He turned around and left…

As their wedding date got closer, Savitri felt a strange sensation. She told herself it was just her nerves. She dreamt of death and being alive in a grave with a dead woman, thorns ripping at her sides.

Two weeks later, she mentioned her dreams to Rahim. He smiled. "You frightened to be tied to me."

Maybe he was right, it was just nerves.

"Finally, I am getting married," she was saying to her mother as she stepped into the church.

Two days after the wedding party, Savi was feeling "woozy and fatigued."

"I told you, that last dance with your old boyfriend," Rahim winked.

But even after a refreshing bath, a good old village breakfast, and an easy morning by late evening, she was dragging like a mule that carried double its usual load up a hill. They postponed their honeymoon for a couple of days.

As the week moved along, she felt even worse, and her overwhelming sense of fear came back. She even swore that she smelled like a rotting dog and her toes were turning black. She got weak and could barely walk. Rahim was worried by now; he could not find any medical explanation for her condition. He took her to specialist clinics. The doctors were baffled by this unexplained illness. The blackness that started showing in her toes had now spread up to Savitri's calves, the skin on her calves was shrivelling, little bumps were rising on her calves. These bumps swelled and popped; maggots crawled out of these holes. She got weaker and weaker. She was hospitalized; her whole body was rotting while she was very much alive. Doctors thought about every illness under the sun and tried everything they could, nothing worked.

The rotten dog scent was now a pervading presence, and it permeated the ward. She had to be isolated. Pus, mucus, and maggots seeped from her body. Blackened flesh jumped off her body in chunks, leaving gaping craters of green and black holes and maligned flesh behind. Pain and agony were her companions.

As she laid there in her foggy state, Savi heard, "The dead is living in you," a woman was in her room. "Listen, somebody tie you to the dead," she disappeared as fast as she had appeared.

By now, Savi couldn't even put a coherent sentence together and she always had on an oxygen mask. She just assumed that this was death coming for her.

This woman was not death, she was a cleaner at the hospital, one of those ancient types. She saw the works of evil on Savitri. The next day she waited for Savi's family in the car park and hoped that they would listen to her because Savi's time on earth would be cut short if they did not take heed.

The little old woman that approached them was harmless and Rahim knew she worked in the hospital, so they stopped for a quick chat with her despite the challenge they were facing.

"Do you believe in bad eye and evil spirits?"

Savi's parents were all ears, but Rahim was skeptical about this 'obeah talk.' after all, he was a doctor, for him there must be another explanation other than the spirit world.

The woman did not go into details, but she stated, "she could only get better by spiritual help, allyuh medicine can't do nothing for she."

She looked squarely at Rahim. He felt like it was as if she could see what he was thinking.

After a bit of skepticism from Rahim, the family sought the help of the healer.

"The girl ketch a tie from somebody."

He confirmed Savi was suffering from an evil force within her body, which would kill her if it was not removed.

Rahim, at that moment he looked at his love, his life, and a voice spoke to his inner core, "believe and your love can save her." He nodded to the healer, who was staring at him.

"Bring her tomorrow morning, I will send Marva to get you," pointing to Rahim he said, "Only you come."

The next day, Marva showed up before the sun woke; Rahim was ready.

The healer, Papa Boi, lived off Parrrylands, at the end of Guapo village, heading into the forested area. They had to park on the outskirts and walk to his house.

As a child, Rahim was not as adventurous as others. He never ventured down these parts. But he remembered tales about Papa Boi, who seemed to be around since his dearly departed grandparents' days.

Marva stopped at the entrance. "Only you can go on from here," she patted him on his back and left.

'Lord, what I get myself in,' the fleeting panic evaporated when he looked down at what remained of his wife in his arms. He stepped inside. Papa Bois's house was a wood and mud tepee shaped structure with dried coconut branches weaved together for a roof and mud flooring. Strange paintings, stones, wooden artifacts, dried branches of this and that were hanging from the walls. Bottles of liquids with suspicious looking elements swimming in them were laid out on a huge rough handmade wooden table. Rahim felt as if he had stepped into the universe three thousand years ago. Papa Boi was dressed in some kind of animal skin gown, his face painted like a native Arawak.

He took Savitri from Rahim's arms and pointed to a spot in a corner, where Rahim assumed he was to go to, so he did. Papa Boi laid Savi down on a bed of earth surrounded by candles in the middle of the room and began moving around in a circle, chanting. He sounded like the Baptist worshippers talking in tongues when they 'ketch a spirit.' Savitri spoke, the voice that came from her mouth did not belong to her.

Rahim felt the pores and hairs on his body rise. The voice related a tale from the chambers of a grave.

It said, "Sumintra (Savitri's cousin) is jealous of Savitri because she wants Rahim, and she put me in a dead woman and tie Savitri. I must kill Savitri to be set free; the woman, Miss Ann Walker, is buried in the La Pre cemetery."

Rahim's head was making revolutions around the planet; he knew the contents of his small meal from yesterday were soon going to be on the floor.

Papa Boi continued his utterings. There was a loud rumbling sound. Savitri's stomach raised, her body jerked upwards, her mouth opened.

Woosh!

A wind came, blew out the candles, shocked the house and the earth beneath Rahim's feet vibrated as a screeching from the pits of Hades emanated from Savi's mouth. The spirit spoke no more, Savi's body slumped down to the earth.

Rahim was just about to faint when Papa Boi caught him

"It almost over."

Rahim peeked over at Savi. He was almost sure that she was looking a little better.

Papa Boi whispered, "don't worry, she go be ok."

He gave Rahim a concoction to drink and went on "When somebody go to a obeah man to make obeah on you, he make the person who envy you take clothes with your sweat, hair, fingernail, or anything like that. Then he connect with a spirit and trap it. The obeah man dig up a grave at night and put the clothes and spirit in the mouth ah a fresh dead. When he put the item and spirit in the dead mouth, he sew it up with a chant over the body and then cover the grave. The dead person is one with the living, as the spirit try to get free the living person rot away just like the body rot in the grave. The living dies when the spirit break free ah the dead body."

Papa Bois said, "For now, I in control ah the spirit but I have to reverse the curse."

The only way to stop the curse was to dig up the dead, remove whatever was used, burn it, wash the body of the sick person, and pour the water into the dead mouth, then perform rituals to cast of the spell and lay the dead to rest.

Papa Bois told Rahim, "Go home."

His legs refused to cooperate with his brain. "Oh God

"You have to trust and believe in what you can't see, son, to save her."

"Beep! It is three am!"

The alarm was useless noise, his eyes did not close, the night gone by. On', his return to Papa Bois's Savi was just as he left her. Papa Bois bundled Savi into animal skin and placed her in the car. They left, heading to the village an hour away.

On arriving there, they searched for the relatives of the dead woman and explained what had happened. Rahim prayed for divine intervention. He knew if they did not believe, Savi had no chance. Since they needed the relatives' permission to go to the cemetery. Luck was on their side, Anna Walker's widow; James recalled the night after his wife's burial.

"Sweet Jesus, I went to the cemetery that night. I thought I saw people by Anna's grave. The wreaths were scattered…"

It was already the hour when people stayed clear of burial grounds, hopefully no one would see them. Rahim carried a bottle of water Papa Bois had prepared for this event to the graveside, and then he and James scooted back to the car.

Papa Bois placed Savitri on the ground, dug up the grave, and slipped into it. He retrieved the garment from the corpse's mouth. Burnt it, poured some of the water on the ashes and the rest on Savi. Collected a little of the water by squeezing the animal skin around her into the bottle. He poured it into the dead woman's mouth. He covered the grave, did his chant, and went back to the car with Savitri in his arms.

Papa Bois chanting his tongues, got into the backseat with Savi and off they went, taking James to his home. Rahim thanked James for his help and James wished them the best.

Papa Bois chanted until they got back to his house. When they got there, he placed Savitri on the ground. Savi woke up as fresh as the morning rose. She didn't remember a thing.

As they were leaving, Papa Bois held out a newspaper clipping. It was a young Papa Bois, MD class of 75, Oxford University. Rahim was speechless.

Papa Bois smiled. "See the grave you passing in the yard? That is my Elizabeth, I didn't believe. It was too late for her by the time I did. Not everything in life could be explained with logic or science."

Ma Clar The Village Santiwah

A non-fiction tribute to my grandmother

"…But yuh cyar ketch me," the Mighty Sparrow warns his would-be wife Melda in the eponymous calypso, "with necromancy. / All you do cyar get thru;/ ah still eh go marrid to you."

Doctor Bird's self-assurance derives, we discover, from the fact that "Papa Neza is my grandfather." But had Melda had the good fortune, like me, to be the granddaughter of Ma Clar, Sparrow's smugness might well have proven to be misplaced. In her heyday, "Miss Wells," as she was known, was renowned and revered as the village healer, visiting the sick and binding the dead, giving healing baths to the suffering, making soothing balms for those in pain and delivering babies where they were wanted and dispatching them where, as in the case of the proper young lady who had got herself into trouble down by the river or elsewhere, they were not. In simple terms, she ran a 24-hour unofficial clinic. Her specialties bush medicine, planting, and cooking.

The granddaughter of ex-slaves with certified Yoruba roots, Clarissa "Ma Clar" Wells, née David, grew up on a cocoa estate in Grenada with 13 siblings. At eighteen, she arrived in Trinidad, barefooted, unschooled, and hungry but armed with an asset, an extensive knowledge of Caribbean herbs and spices and their salutary and culinary properties. This art of traditional healing, often disparagingly referred to as "bush medicine" by the skeptical and the uninitiated, had been passed down through generations of her Yoruba ancestors and eagerly assimilated by the young lady who had had the good fortune not to have had her education, in the famous words of George Bernard Shaw, "interrupted while she was in school."

Soon married to Conrad "Papio" Wells, the son of a white plantation owner and a cocoa payol or mulatto mother, who had worked as a maid on the estate in Grenada, Ma Clar worked as a maid, pharmacy help and baby-sitter for a few years in the deep South where the couple had settled. It was not long before they were able to acquire several parcels of estate land in Chaguanas and South: including a 20-acre estate in Cap-de-Ville Point Fortin.

Together, Ma Clar and her husband raised eight children while successfully running the flourishing estate where they grew cocoa, coffee, and citrus and reared ducks, chicken, and livestock, mainly pigs. They set up a depot or meat shop on the main road and, with the proceeds of their industry, they were able to send many of their children abroad to England and North America to enjoy the formal education without which Ma Clar had been able to "make something of myself."

But it was hard work. A strong, dedicated woman, Ma Clar worked in the fields from 3am or 4am every morning, digging yam, harvesting, sunning, milling, and grinding cocoa and coffee to produce the final refined product for sale. She also ran the depot, butchering the pigs and killing, plucking, and cleaning chickens and ducks.

By mid-afternoon every day, her service in the fields finally finished, she moved on to her secondary occupation, becoming the village bush doctor or medicine and rubbing woman, sometimes unkindly called the "obeah woman."

Ma Clar is a woman of great intelligence, with a vast knowledge of herbs and oils and the working of the human body. She also brings to the table the mystical secrets of the African healer. As I walk through the estate grounds with her, I am amazed by the sheer breadth of her knowledge; there is, it seems, not a single bush whose name she does not know, providing comprehensive and precise explanations of its uses. The sometimes-exotic names like zebapique, kuzay maho, vervine, roll easily off her tongue but only one has taken root in the space between the ears on which the names have often fallen.

The house my father grew up in is now used to store bush medicine and spices; dry corn fish, put cocoa balls to dry out, make sugar cake, beni ball, red plum in buckets; grind corn for chili bibi and make toolum with molasses from the big rum barrel. Ma Clar carries all this to the market with other things from the field and closer to Christmas she slaughters and sells the animals too - the pig and duck and chicken that is over the river in the pig pens.

In the evenings and on weekends, we would run wild, bathe in the river, ketch river crab and boil them in empty milk pan, feast on mangoes, oranges, pois doux, jackfruit, pick the vegetables and water the crotons, hibiscus, and palms. Weekend ritual. We went to the spa at Ma Clar's— "a good bush bath, then, she drown we in coconut oil and homemade chicken fat grease; rub we down and bend we up all how to straighten we nose; we leg and stretch we body. And a good dose ah castor oil, shark oil and salts to ward off all sickness."

At Christmas time we learnt the art of baking in a stone oven and cooking on a wood fire. The best meat that we ever ate; Ma Clar's secret spice and herb rub grinded in the mill and finished up with the mortar and pestle, patted into the meat and then she would, "slow roast in fig leaves."

Today, my son looks at me in amazement as I pick senna leaves and pound them with my mortar and pestle and put these in the half of barrel with water outside, along with baking soda, lime, rosemary, black sage leaves, red lavender. I let it *cusumay* for a few hours in the hot sun: I dunk my squealing granddaughter into the barrel. Following up her bath with a coconut oil rubdown.

"Ma, he laughs, "you and this old bush thing."

I smile, "best thing I ever learnt from my grandmother, bush thing and cooking."

Credits

Public Lies, Private Lives: An Untold Story of a Coup – Winner of Hodder Education The Island Voices: Caribbean Contemporary Classics Short Story Competition

Coup Time: Town on Fire- shortlisted for Alpine Fellowship writing International Prize 2024

Town on Fire- longlisted for Bridport International Short Story Prize 2024

Chronicles of a Compound Child- first published in Solarpunk Magazine Issue #3

Bam Bam See Am Look Thing! -International Literary Seminars (ILS) Fellowship Award 2023

Ashes from 1990: A Daughter's Downfall- first published in The Caribbean Writer Vol. 38

Teenaged Coup - first published in Lolwe Magazine issue # 8

114th Muslimean Memory- first published in The Caribbean Writer Vol. 36

Raya - first published by Hodder Education in Island Voices

Rahim and Papa Bois- Semi-finalist for the Kinsman Quarterly Iridescence Awards 2024

Ma Clar The Village Santiwah- Second Place Hammond House International Origins Competition

Illustrations

Front Cover: Painting by Salisha Corbie

Page 8: Maco Mere Fred by Ammaarah Salam

Page 126: ISIS Trinis by Ammaarah Salam